The Prez's Forbidden Temptation

Copyright

Paperback ISBN: 978-1-961966-71-0

Published by: Carxander Publishing
Minnesota

Opening Quote

Baby, tell me where you wanna run. 'Cause I've been burning like the morning sun. Take my hand, you can burn this city with me. Play me like your first guitar. Where every single note's too hard. I don't even care. You can take me there. We can set the world on fire. Baby, you're all I need. Come now, set me free like a wildfire. Breathless, I can't resist. Melt in your scarlet kiss like a wildfire.

Wildfire by Demi Lovato

Chapter One

☪ Blade ☪

"You know, I respect the hell out of you, Prez, but this is the stupidest fucking idea you've ever had," Killian, or as I call him, Racer, says to me. He's the Vice President of Texas' chapter of Viper's Venom, led by me.

Killian is somewhere around six-feet-two. His hair is midnight black and styled religiously in a military-crew cut. He gets it trimmed once a month no matter where we are or what he's doing. His eyes are black as his fucking soul, and the tattoo on his left bicep shows exactly which side of the line of good and evil he's on. It's not God's.

I personally like the pentagram he sports. I especially like the *666* on the underside of his wrist. He's not a satan worshiper. He's just, like me, as unreligious as they fucking come. If there is a God, he's got one sick sense of fucking humor. Maybe that's what makes this thirty-seven-year-old, a year younger than me, my best friend.

Or maybe it's simply because he doesn't take my shit and is the only one I've ever let put me in my place when I'm losing control. Well, other than my little sister.

I take a drink of the whiskey in my glass and close my eyes as I lean back against his couch in his living room. "I don't think so."

"Blade. Come on. You're thirty-eight and acting like a fucking high school kid. You know he's better with you than without. Without, he has to fend for himself."

"Come on, Racer. You know that's not fucking true." I lean forward and rest my elbows on my knees. I shake my head and swirl the amber liquid in its glass. "He's got his cousins. Colton. He's not alone."

"You think a cop is better than you?"

I sigh and finish off my drink. "It's already done. He'll be waking up soon. He'll see the note. He'll be crushed, and that's going to fucking hurt us both, but he's better off without me. Especially with this danger coming at us."

"A danger you still haven't spoken about to anyone but me."

"Ace knows. He'll send backup if he has to." I set my glass on the table and lean back again.

Ace is the president of our entire organization. He has a chapter in Chicago that covers all of Illinois, but he runs everything we do across the nation. If someone fucks up, they answer to him. If they think they'll be able to get away with anything, they have another thing coming. Ace knows fucking everything.

"You know we need to brief people."

"And we will. When Drake is safe."

"And what about after, Blade? What then?"

"Fuck, I haven't drank enough for this line of questioning, asshole. Can I stay here or not?" I growl.

Racer sighs heavily. "Fine. You can stay here, but just know that I'm very much against you on this. Answer the question. What about after?"

"You know damn well how dangerous my job is. I'm better off alone. We all are."

"Huh. Good to know. I'll be sure to tell my girl." His voice is laced with an insane amount of sarcasm. He knows if he does that, Lizzie, his girl and my sister, will kick my fucking ass into next week.

"You're not changing my mind. Drake has his whole damn life ahead of him. He absolutely does not need to be tethered to someone like me who can so easily ruin everything he has going for him."

"Or maybe that's exactly what he needs." Racer gets up and walks down the hall of his quaint-sized home. He comes back a few minutes later and throws a blanket and pillow at me. "Don't wake my kid up. If he wakes up and wakes Lizzie up, I will personally make sure you don't see sunrise."

I chuckle. "You ain't getting a 'yes, sir' out of me. Leave that for your bedroom."

"Don't need one. I'll be getting enough groveling soon when you realize how badly you fucked up." Racer doesn't say another word. He heads upstairs to his bedroom, thankfully leaving me the rest of the bottle of whiskey.

I forgo the glass this time and drink straight from the bottle. The burn of the delicious liquid slides down my throat as I stare out the window. I shut the lamp out and glance at my phone. It's three in the morning. I've only been away from Drake for an hour, and I already hate myself.

The minutes tick by. The bottle gets emptier and emptier until I'm finishing it off. I make sure to drain every last drop. By the time the sun is rising, I'm passing out into a tortured and very restless sleep.

When I wake up, I don't even know how long I've been out, but Racer's four-year-old is in full meltdown mode. He's screaming. The sound pierces not only the sound barrier, but my fucking head. I feel like it's splitting in half.

"Oh shit," I whisper as I sit up. I glance at my phone. The sun has barely risen, which means I've only been asleep for maybe an hour. Not long enough to forget how much I drank or why. I close my eyes and groan low, suddenly being hit with a pillow. My eyes fly open, and I block the next attack, which hits my forearms instead of my face, but fucking barely. "What the hell?"

"You left an open bottle of fucking whiskey on the table, you fucking asshole!" a shrill and very pissed off Lizzie screams.

I look up briefly before I'm covering myself again and blocking her hits. For a pillow, they sure are harder than I would think they could be. Lizzie, despite the fact that she's skinny enough to get blown over by the Texas wind, puts power behind each swing. She might be five-feet-seven and weigh probably half what I do, but she acts like the baddest of all the bikers I've ever come across or have in my crew. No one would

6

ever believe it when they look at her frame, blond hair, and blue eyes. She's exactly the opposite of me or Killian.

I breathe a little relieved when she quits hitting me, but my head feels like thunder is rumbling inside it. "It was empty!" I yell back, covering my face to block a third attack.

She hits me three times with the pillow as she yells. "It still had enough for Cal to drink, you idiot!"

I finally get a hold of the pillow and yank it out of her hands. "Jesus Christ, Lizzie. Calm the fuck down!"

As if my words instantly infuriate her more, she launches at me with another shrill and pissed off scream. "You selfish prick!"

Racer, thankfully, saves me from having to wrestle with his wife and pin her to the fucking couch, but she does get in a kick to my shin as he lifts her off the ground, hauling her away. "Lizzie, enough!" he barks. I groan and rub my leg, glaring at their backs.

"Ugh! Out, Blade!" she screams at me. I glare even harder at her.

"Stop it! Take Cal to school, and get your ass to work! I'm not going to fight your fucking manager when he fucking fires you!"

"Then, maybe I'll just quit! You hate me working anyway!"

"Knock it off, Elizabeth," Racer growls as he sets her down in the kitchen. "It doesn't matter. You love your job, and I'm not taking you away from something you love. You know better. I'll deal with Blade. Go."

"I can't take him to school, Killian! He fucking drank what was left in that bottle!"

"There wasn't anything left! Do you think I didn't check him out before you even got down here and knew what was happening? You're fucking overreacting! He's his fucking uncle! Do you honestly think Blade, your fucking brother by literal blood, would do something so fucking stupid?"

I shoot my sister another glare and growl low. "I do not have the goddamn energy or patience to deal with this shit. There was nothing left in the bottle. I finished it off. I passed out. I'm sorry I didn't toss the bottle, but come the fuck on!" I rub my head and look at Cal, still crying at the table where he had been eating a breakfast it looks like he finished. "Are one of you going to deal with him? Or shall I?"

Lizzie looks at Cal and hurries to him. "I'm sorry, baby. I shouldn't have yelled."

She wraps her arms around him and hugs him. Like a second skin, motherhood snaps right back into place. Lizzie is one of the best people I've had the pleasure of knowing. She's the only one in our family who accepted me and loved me even when our parents kicked me out. She loves being a tattoo artist, but motherhood is what she loves the most.

Cal hugs her and instantly calms. He's a good kid. Smart. He looks exactly like Killian but managed to gain his mother's blond hair and blue eyes. Everyone who has ever seen him knows damn well he's going to be one hell of a heartbreaker when he grows up. He's already got natural swag, and he's only four.

I chance getting up and stumble my way over to her. I wrap my arms around her and Cal. "I'm sorry, Liz. I am. I should've been more careful."

"Please don't do that again. Please. I can't handle what could happen." She puts her arm around me.

I nod. "Promise. I was upset. In my head. I wasn't thinking. I'll be more careful."

"You need to talk to Drake. You know that right?" She pulls away from me and cleans Cal's face up.

"It's not that simple." I shake my head, and regret the movement.

"It is, but you're a man who likes to complicate things."

I chuckle as I stand. "It's not like it's enjoyable. It's how my life fucking works." I walk back to the couch but feel her piercing blue eyes on me the entire time. I sit down carefully before laying on my back and closing my eyes.

"It doesn't have to be, Blade." I hear some shuffling and a door close.

"I'll be at the clubhouse," Racer said. "I have some shit to look into."

"Thanks." I know that shit he's talking about is the mess we're in with yet another rival gang who wants my turf. Who the fuck knows why these little fuckers can't learn from the larger gangs out there, like Hell's Angels. They leave us alone. We leave them alone. It's simple. Less fighting. Less bloodshed.

8

I sigh and pull the blanket back up as I turn to my side. My head is still spinning like a motherfucker, and all I want to do is pass out. I stare at my phone after Racer leaves. I scrub a hand over my face. Drake should be awake and about to head out for his run. Probably saw the note. Maybe he texted.

I reach for it, my heart racing. When I see no messages or calls, my chest tightens in both utter disappointment and unadulterated relief.

But I can't stop myself from putting my phone on the couch next to me. My background is a picture of me and Drake. I'm sitting on my Harley. Drake is sitting between my legs with his head turned towards me. Our lips are close, and we're looking deeply in each other's eyes. Lizzie snapped that picture and sent it to me. I kissed him the very next moment. It was our first. Many came after that.

Drake is my whole world. Walking out of that room and leaving him was the hardest thing I've ever done in my life. He's a couple of inches shorter than me. He's six-feet-two, muscular, and has a runner's body. He plays Wide Receiver on the Brystone Springs College football team. He's part of the All-Stars, which include all of his cousins, who also play on the team.

I'd hoped for a lifetime with him, but that was a very stupid thing to wish. Men like me don't get fairytale endings. Our endings are dark. Horror film endings, and usually just as bloody.

I won't let that happen to him, but his cappuccino-colored eyes will haunt my nights and days for the rest of my life.

Chapter Two

☾ Drake ☾

"How was your day at school, honey?" my mom, Gladys Remington, asks me. She's named after her grandmother, who she loves dearly still to this day, even though she's been gone since just after I was born almost seventeen years ago.

"It was good. Practice felt long, but I think that was because Coach kept running the defense on plays. He kept saying they need to catch up to the offensive line's skill. We were all just sitting there cheering them on. Felt a little boring, though. I wanted to run through a couple plays with Sterling."

"Well, I'm sure he'll let you tomorrow," my dad, Decker Remington, says.

"Yeah, I'm sure." I turn my head to look out at the fields we're passing. "Where are we going?"

"Me and your dad have a surprise for you," Mom says.

I grin. "What is it?"

"You'll see when we get there," Dad says. I grin even wider and start looking around the vehicle. I see a duffle bag behind me and reach for it.

"No cheating, Mister!" Mom barks.

I laugh and teasingly reach for it anyway. "But I bet what's in here would tell me where we're going."

Dad laughs. "It would. Which is why you can't touch it."

Mom reaches around and swats my leg with a smile. "Behave." She starts to turn back around as I laugh. "We're almost there any- Look out!" she suddenly screams.

My eyes dart to the front windshield just as Dad swerves to miss a pickup truck that's coming straight at us. Only it's in our lane and about to hit us head on. I brace for the hit. I'm sitting in the back on the passenger's side. Mom is in front of me. Dad is driving. He yanks the wheel to the right so he'll take the brunt of the hit. It's a two lane road, and there's a semi in the other lane. I see immediately it's best to take the impact from the pickup.

He tries to avoid contact with the pickup and hit the side of the road or ditch instead, but the pickup seemingly picks up speed. I see the crazed, bloodshot eyes of the driver just as he slams into the side of our car. I brace myself as the car starts flipping. I hear the glass shattering; Mom screaming; Dad cursing.

There's so much josling. Like time slows down to a crawl, I feel my seat belt snapping. The next thing I know, I'm flying through the air. The ground gets closer and closer.

Pavement.

I hear something. A pop-pop.

What is that?

I hit the ground with a thud. I feel the side of my head bounce off it; bones breaking.

Everything is instantly pitch black.

I sit up in bed panting and feeling my body. My head. Torso. Everything I can touch. I throw the covers off and feel my legs. I'm sweating. The nightmare plays over and over again in my mind, slowly fading as the seconds pass like the end of an old movie.

After a few minutes, my heart begins to slow. My eyes wide, I flop back down on the bed and stare at the ceiling. Like I was slapped with frigid water, I'm completely awake.

"Fuck," I whisper. "Just a dream. Holy fuck." It takes me a few minutes to come back to myself. When I finally do, I glance at the clock. I can see the sun has just risen, but probably barely. The clock tells me it's almost 7AM, which means I overslept and don't have time for my morning run. "Shit." I reach for Blade. "Blade, I gotta go. I'm gonna be late."

I don't feel him in the bed, so I turn and look at the side he sleeps on. He's not in it, and the sheets feel cold, telling me he's already been up for quite a while. That explains why his arms aren't around me like they usually would be. I sit up again and look around the bedroom. We fell asleep a little late last night. I didn't expect he'd be up before me.

I see the bathroom door is slightly ajar. Light is coming through the small crack. I sigh on a long breath. I was worried he took off somewhere early, but I'm grateful to know he didn't. I need him right now. That nightmare fucking shook me.

It's not like I haven't had it before. It's recurring. I have it a lot. It's more of a remembrance dream. My own demon's way of not letting me forget the way I lost my parents that day.

Like I could ever forget it anyway. It took awhile for all the details to come back to me, but now I remember everything that happened like it's happening all over again. I feel the glass shattering all around me, cutting my skin, just as if it was doing it every time the images cross through my mind, which is more often than I'd like. I remember the smells, the pain of hitting the hot asphalt of the road, everything that was said during the drive. Everything I did and didn't do.

I often torture myself by asking what I could've done differently. Maybe if I hadn't been messing around, they would've seen the truck earlier. Or if they hadn't been taking me wherever they were, it wouldn't have happened. Thoughts like that are running through my head all of the time. The only person who really knows what I truly think is Blade. I live with a lot of guilt that I was the only survivor, though no one knows how. I should've died that day.

And Kody. After my parent's death, Kody's parent's took me in. All of my cousin's would've, but I've always been close to Kody. He's more than just my best friend and cousin. Kody is like a brother to me.

After a few minutes of silence, I realize the shower isn't running. No water is running. There's no sound coming from the bathroom at all. I get up slowly and grab a pair of boxers out of my overnight bag. I spend just as much time at Blade's house on the Viper's Venom compound as I do at Kody's place. The only difference is I don't have a drawer or closet space here. Blade has been very cautious of a lot of things lately, me moving in especially.

This is something we've been talking about for quite a while, only I wasn't eighteen then. I turned eighteen last year. I'm nineteen now. Blade has spent the entire last year back and forth on when the right time for us to be together is. We've already been together since the day my parents died. He was the first one on scene. I wouldn't be here if not for him. He saved my life.

So, why things have been a rollercoaster with him is something I'm not okay with and can't make sense of. Every time I try to bring it up, though, something happens, and he needs to leave.

Fuck. Maybe it's not the right time. I don't even know anymore. I'm still not thinking straight after that dream.

"Blade?" I ask, knocking on the bathroom door. "You in there?" I'm met with nothing but silence, so I push the door open a little bit. My heart pounds because I don't know what I'm going to find. Blade on the floor?

But no one is in the bathroom. It's just as it was left last night after we cleaned up from our romp under the sheets. I lean against the doorframe bewildered for a few moments before I go in and take a quick shower. Maybe he's at the clubhouse or something.

After quickly running through my morning routine and getting dressed, I catch a glimpse of something out of the corner of my eye. I chuckle when I realize it's a note he left on his pillow. I was too shaken to even see it, but I should've known he'd give me something. Sometimes, it's a text. Sometimes, a note. He never just takes off without telling me where he's going, though.

I sit on the bed smiling softly as I open the note, but the words I read stop my breathing and cease my heart from beating.

Dray,

We need to break this off once and for all, baby. I don't want you getting hurt, and the longer we're together, the higher the likelihood of that happening is.

I hope you understand that I can't be the reason you lose your life. I need you safe, and if that means you being as far from me as possible, then that's what I'll do.

You'll always own my heart.

Blade

I reread the letter again and again. With each passover, I become more and more angry. I'm not letting him do this without talking to me face to face. I grab my duffel bag and crumble the note in my hand before stuffing it in my pocket. If space is what he needs to decide he's being stupid about this, I'll give it to him, but if he thinks this is over without a real conversation, he has another thing coming. I don't care that he's the President of Viper's Venom here in Texas. He needs me as much as I need him.

I head downstairs and leave his house. I slam his door behind me and jog to the clubhouse. When I get there, I open the door with enough force to have a couple guys looking at me surprised. I don't say a word and they don't dare. I storm directly to Blade's office.

"Well, I don't think it's a great idea either, but he won't tell me what the fuck has him acting like this," someone says just as I'm turning the corner and entering the office.

"Where's Blade?" I grunt at Racer. He's Blade's best friend, brother-in-law, Viper's Venom's Vice President, and Blade's second in command. The guy he's talking to is Axel. An enforcer. Big guy. Blonde. He has a scar on his face from a knife fight, and a tattoo on his neck. A few on his arms. Not someone I'd want to meet in a dark alley.

Racer sits down in Blade's chair behind his desk. "I don't know, man. He's got a lot on his mind. He won't talk to me."

I narrow my eyes. I know damn well he knows where Blade is. Blade doesn't go anywhere without telling him. "Come on, Racer. I've been 'round longer than that. Where the fuck is he?"

"Drake, I can't tell you that, man. I can't. Just know that I'm on your fucking side on this. I'll work on it. Just give him space to realize he's a fucking idiot."

14

We both stare each other down. Axel has the smarts to not try to intervene because I'm not sure I'd be able to hold back swinging a fist at his jaw. After a few moments, I finally sigh. "What the hell is his deal, Racer? Everything was fine last night."

"I wish I had answers for you, man. I don't. Just let me work on it. Get out of here. You have school. It rained last night. I parked your car in the garage here at the clubhouse after you guys went back to Blade's. He really needs to clean out his garage."

I roll my eyes. "I don't see that happening. He likes fixing bikes and cars up too much."

Racer tosses me my keys, and I head outside, still pissed the hell off. I throw my bag in the passenger seat and get in the driver's seat of my red, convertible Mustang GT. It's brand new and my baby.

I start it up and back out of the garage, careful not to hit anyone's bike. Before I take off, though, I text Blade.

Drake: You and I aren't done. I'm not giving you up, and you have a whole other thing coming if you think for a single second it's over. It's not over. Forever and Always, baby. Me and you against the world. I don't care if it's burning to the ground around us. We're meant for each other. We love each other. And it's not over.

I put my phone down, put my car in gear, and take off at a rate of speed I know I shouldn't be driving.

But fuck it, right?

Maybe it's time to live a little dangerously.

Chapter Three

☾ Blade ☾

(One Week Later)

I squint my eyes, unsure what I'm seeing in front of me. A crash? I start slowing down. The closer I get, the more I can see what's going on.

"Oh, shit!" I say as I watch in horror. A car flips a few times into a ditch. A truck skids to a stop and what looks like two people jump out. Did they hit them?

I speed up so I can get to the scene quicker. Maybe I can help. The rumble of the engine of my Harley as I accelerate purrs underneath me. I love my bike. It's Navy blue with chrome and an American flag painted on it. Of all the bikes I've owned, this one has always been my favorite, and I've had it the longest.

By the time I get to the scene, the truck is speeding away, but I know it's two males. Hillbillies, complete with backwards caps and farmer's tans. I memorize the plate as they speed away and I stop. TX7190.

"Has to be personalized," I grumble as I get off my bike to survey the scene. Maybe the numbers are significant.

The second my eyes land on him, I know I just walked into something very dangerous. I immediately take out my phone and run to the kid laying sprawled facedown on the pavement as I'm dialing 911.

I kneel next to him as the phone rings. I feel for a pulse, and he groans low.

"911, what's your emergency?" a woman who sounds very young answers.

"I need emergency on County Road HH. Now. There's been a crash."

"A crash? How many vehicles, sir?"

"There were two. One drove away. It was a beat up Dodge Ram. Don't know the year, but it didn't look new. License plate is TX7190. Two males. Both looked to be mid-thirties and wearing jeans, dark in color, and t-shirts. Driver was wearing red. Passenger was wearing white. Both had hats. Backwards. Both were wearing something to hide their face. They sped off heading West."

"Hit and run. Okay, sir. Do you know if anyone is in the other vehicles? Injuries?"

I look down at the kid. "I don't want to move him, but there's a kid in his teens. Probably about sixteen to eighteen. Looks like he was ejected from the car. The car's on fire. I don't know how many occupants or their injuries."

"Emergency is on the way. Can you look at the others? Is the teen breathing?"

"Teen is breathing. Looks to be pretty severely injur-" I'm cut off by a large explosion. My body automatically curls over the kid to protect him as I glance over my shoulder. "Fuck! The car exploded!" I cover the kid as much as I can as debris rains down around us.

"Okay. Okay, sir," the woman says. I can hear the panicked edge in her voice. "Um... I... have emergency on the way. Can you tell me more about where you are?"

"West of town, ma'am," I say, keeping my voice as calm as possible, sensing she's new and needs it. "West of Brystone Springs. About three miles out."

"Thank you, sir." She takes a deep breath, and I know the 'thank you' is for the information given and for keeping calm and helping her to be.

I look up when I see a vehicle approaching. I can't let this kid stay in the middle of the road like this, but when I see the same vehicle I saw take off just moments ago, I know something big is going down. "Oh fuck," I whisper.

"What?" the woman asks, alarmed.

I ignore her and look down at the kid. He's moving a little. "Kid, I need you to get up. We need to move."

"Mmrph...," he groans.

The truck is getting closer, but they've slowed down considerably. "I'm taking the kid to the hospital. Now."

"What? Sir, my ambulance is not far."

"Now, ma'am." I put my phone on speaker and make a snap decision. "I really hope I don't fuck you up even more, kid." As gently as I can, I lift the kid in my arms. I quickly move to my bike and get on, still cradling him. "Christ. You need to hold on, kid. Hold onto me."

"Sir! What's going on?"

"Hold onto me, man. Come on."

"Sir!"

I glance over my shoulder just as the teen in my arms grips the waistband of my jeans. I look down at him. His dark hair falls over his eyes. He groans once more, but he's holding on. "Good. Good boy." The truck seems to be slowing a lot more, but he's watching me. "If you want that truck," I say into my phone, "you better get a squad to meet me somewhere. I'm heading to the hospital and coming in hot."

I hang up before she can say anything more and keep my eyes on the truck. The driver's and passenger's eyes are focused on me, almost like they're challenging me. I chuckle as I put my phone back in my pocket. I start my motorcycle and quickly make a u-turn. I gun the engine and head back to town.

I feel the teen grip me tighter, and I'm thankful he's conscious enough to do it. I couldn't explain why his touch drives me crazy. I don't know why I feel like I'm on fucking cloud nine as I race through down the road, leaving the truck chasing me in my dust.

About a mile from city limits, I see two squads racing towards the scene. I slow my speed, though I'm still traveling well over the limit. As I hoped, the truck catches up quickly, but it's too late for him. An unmarked squad car is coming towards us and whips around behind him, lights and sirens blaring. I take off once more and navigate my way through the streets of our small town until I reach the hospital.

I stop in front of the emergency exit and keep the kid in my arms as I run in the doors. My heart is beating out of my chest, and I already know I'm not going anywhere until I know he's okay.

"Drake!" I yell as I jerk awake and nearly fall off the couch in my office where I've been spending most of my time. I feel like I'm choking. My mouth is dry, and I'm out of breath. I feel like I just ran a marathon. "Shit…," I whisper, rubbing my chest as the door to my office opens. It's dark, and I squint at the light that suddenly pours into the room.

"You okay, Prez?" Axel asks me.

"Yeah. Yeah. Fine."

He looks hesitant. "Uh… You sure? This is the third time this week you've woken up screaming Drake's name."

I sigh. "I'm fine. Really." I lay back down. "What the hell time is it?"

"Almost six. I was coming to wake you up so we could head out to follow up on that lead."

"I'll be out in a few minutes."

"Okay."

We figured out that our trouble gang is staying on the outskirts on the other side of town. I want to take them out today, but I need to observe the fuckers first. They aren't even a MC. They're just a bunch of fucking young, immature assholes who thought it would be cool to start a gang and create chaos. My problem, though, is they've caught the attention of a much larger gang. So, now I need to protect these assholes from a much larger problem that we don't need in our town.

And it's that much larger problem that had me pushing Drake away in the first place. I don't want him near these guys. They're a dangerous Latin American gang trying to establish themselves in Texas. I was hoping other Latin gangs would just eradicate them, but all they did is push them closer to me. They tend to go after loved ones of the gangs they're fighting.

I scrub my hands over my face as I get up. I head for the bathroom and take a few minutes to clean up. Once I finish, I grab my cuts and head outside. Everyone is already gathered.

"How do you wanna do this, Blade?" Racer asks.

19

I'm just about to answer when my phone signals that I have an incoming message. I sigh and take my phone out. I know who it is. I don't have to look. Drake wasn't kidding when he said he wasn't giving up. He's sent me several texts over the week that have broke me more and more. I know I'm doing the right thing right now. I have to protect him, but he's not making it easy. He texts me every single morning that he loves me and misses me. The only difference today from the others is that he's added that he's tired of messing around and that we need to talk.

I put my phone away, my heart breaking into more pieces. "Full force. Surround them. I want them to know they have our attention."

I climb on my bike. Flashes of Drake wrapped around me invade my mind, but I shake them off. Nothing has changed. I can't be the reason he loses his life. I'd never forgive myself for that.

So, I ride.

I let the wind blow through my short brown hair.

And I try to forget about the man who owns my heart.

Only, his eyes haunt me. They're everywhere I am. I see them when I'm awake, and when I close my eyes.

Drake is my entire life. I hate that I have to live it without him, but he deserves one that doesn't involve him having to look over his shoulder all of the time.

Drake deserves to be happy. To have everything he's ever wanted in life.

Even if that's without me.

Chapter Four

☪ Drake ☪

(One Week Later)

Pop! Pop!

I lay as still as possible. It's not hard. Every bone in my body hurts. Every muscle. Every pore of my being.

I don't know what that was. Gunshots?

I hear a roar.

It gets louder and louder until it's right on top of me. I keep my eyes closed and don't dare breathe. My lungs scream at me to give them any tiny bit of air I can, but I refuse.

I hear an engine start before a vehicle speeds off. The truck that hit us? Are they just leaving us? What the fuck was that popping noise?

My heart speeds up until all I can hear is it thundering in my skull. I vaguely hear someone's voice.

"Accident...," a deep voice says. It instantly soothes me. "County..." His voice seems to cut in and out before some kind of explosion near me seems to deafen me even more. Suddenly, all I can hear is a high-pitch ringing. Like a teapot is going off in my brain.

I groan, and then feel like I'm flying in the air. Am I dead? Did I succumb?

"Hold onto me," that soothing voice says.

Hold on. Hold onto him. I can do it. I know I can. I will my body to obey because I trust that he's here to help. Moments after I get a grip on him, I hear the roaring again. I turn my face into his chest and melt into his woodsy and masculine smell.

Safe. I'm safe.

My eyes jerk open, and I grip my blankets like they're the only things keeping me from drowning. "Blade!" I shout as I sit up, the popping sound still fresh and at the forefront of my mind.

I pant, gripping my chest.

Popping. I don't remember that from before. Was that something that happened before the car exploded? Did I hear it catching on fire? Would it sound that loud? Like gunshots?

I take breath after breath and glance at the door when it opens. A shadow steps inside and closes the door behind it. It takes me a moment to realize I'm not still dreaming.

"You doing okay, bro?" Kody asks as he sits down.

"Not really," I admit.

Kody sighs and crawls into bed with me. Without saying a word he hugs me. "It's still early."

"I know."

"You should try getting some more sleep. You haven't been getting a lot these past two weeks."

"Kind of hard to do when Blade won't answer any of my texts or calls."

"I know. But he has to have a reason. We just need to get down to figuring out why and what's going on. What he's not telling you."

"Easier said than done. Has Colt said anything? Or X?"

"They mentioned there's a gang on the other side of town. But they haven't been causing too many problems because VV went out there last week. I guess they scared them."

I shake my head. "I just don't understand what the fuck is happening. That didn't sound like a fucking goodbye letter to me."

"I know. I read it. It sounded like it pained him to do what he was doing. He didn't seem to want to." Kody hugs me tighter. I'm trying really

22

hard not to break down. Fuck knows I've done enough of that lately. Kody has been through it all with me.

"Maybe I need to just go out there. I wanted to give him space to come to his damn senses, but fuck, this is getting ridiculous."

Kody glances at the clock on my nightstand. "Maybe we should go for a run before practice."

I chuckle. "You mean maybe I should go for a run. You know it clears my head. And you hate running before practice."

Kody grins. "True. But I'd do it for you."

"Actually, I think you're right. I need to work off this dream anyway."

"I was gonna ask about that." Like the brother he's become, he keeps his arm around me. A show of love and our bond. He knows I need the comfort, even though I'd never say it.

"It was the accident. Blade taking off with me. Except this time, I heard pops. Distinct. Like a gunshot. I don't remember them. I mean, I didn't remember them. Not from that day, but I do. I remember them very well now. It wasn't just a dream. They really happened. I must've blocked them. I remember how scared I was. It wasn't long after that the car exploded. I don't know if it was gunshots or the fire, but I remember it happened before Blade got there."

"Hmm… Might be something worth mentioning to Colt. Maybe he could look into it more. There were a lot of unanswered questions around that day."

"Yeah," I say as I look down. After a few moments, I sigh. "Maybe you're right. A run should clear my head."

Kody grins. "Good idea. Want me to call Colt?"

"Don't wake him up. It's not even five yet."

Kody barks out a laugh. "You know he's already up."

I grin. "Okay, true. Yeah, if you want to. Just tell him I'll talk to him later."

"You got it." Kody gives me another hug before he gets up and heads for the door.

I slip out of bed with a sigh and make my way to the bathroom. After brushing my teeth and doing my morning business, I throw a pair of jogging pants on with a t-shirt. I slide some socks on and find my airpods. I find my jogging playlist as I'm heading downstairs to put on my shoes.

Just stepping outside into the fairly cool air makes me feel better. I'm glad I'm doing this before sunrise. Texas heat sucks sometimes.

The longer I run, the better I feel. Before I know it, I'm nearing the park I usually turn around at. It's around three miles from my house on the running trail I'm on. The trail goes through a wooded area that's incredibly peaceful and serene to me. It probably is for most runners. It's a very well used trail. Kody and I have run on it many times ourselves. I've run it with Blade, too.

As soon as I reach the park and start to turn around, my eyes catch sight of a few younger adults not much older than me. They aren't in the park, just on the outskirts near the trail, but I immediately get a bad feeling. I don't say anything as I quickly turn and start heading back the way I came.

"Hey! You!" one of them says in an accent very much not from around here. Sounds a little like Mexico. I'm pretty sure it's that small gang Kody mentioned before I left. I don't want anything to do with them.

I pump my legs. I know I'm fast. It's what makes me so good on the field. I doubt I'll have a problem outrunning these guys.

What I don't count on, though, is a stabbing pain on the outside of my left leg. I stumble and trip before crashing to the ground. My hand instantly goes to my leg. I feel something wet and sticky. Shakily, I hold my hand up to my face.

Blood.

I try to get up, but they're on me before I can. Five of them.

One of them kicks me hard in the stomach. "Think you can just get away like that, huh, All-Star?" He kicks me again.

I know if I don't fight, I'm not getting out of this one alive, so I punch at the leg kicking me as hard as possible. I hear a crack followed by a scream of pain. It allows me just enough time to get back on my feet, but the second I put weight on my leg, I nearly crumble again. Blood is gushing. I realize then that one of them threw a knife, and it's still sticking out of my thigh.

"What the fuck? All-Star came for a fight!"

"Ah! Get him! Fuck!" the one I punch screams as he holds his leg.

Once again, they're all on me. I throw punches and do whatever I can to stay upright. If I fall again, I'm done for. I take as many hits as I give, only mine are harder and connecting different. I hear a few bones break. Screams. Howls of pain.

My knuckles are bloodied. Adrenaline is pumping through my veins at such a high rate, I feel a little like The Flash with how quickly I'm able to move. When someone grabs me from behind, I use them to stabilize me enough to kick at the others with my good leg. I don't dare remove the knife. I know enough about first aid to know that pulling something out of somewhere can cause a lot more damage, even a bleedout. I'm at least two and a half miles from home. I ran for quite a ways before the knife hit.

"Fuck!" one of them shouts as my foot connects hard to his balls. His face instantly turns blue.

"Enough of this shit!" the guy holding me barks as I struggle against him. I elbow him in the ribcage and see a gun in his hand. "Stop fucking squirming!"

I drop my weight at the same time I grab the barrel of the gun, keeping my hand away from the muzzle. Blade taught me how to disarm someone quickly and efficiently. I grab his arm between mine, holding it to my body, and move the gun away from us both, effectively bending his wrist up and out. This allows me to control him and disarm him. It also makes it easy to break, which I'm happy to do.

The satisfying snap brings forth a scream of pain as he lets go of me. One of the others is coming for me again, but I point the gun right at his head as I back up. I don't even feel the knife protruding from my skin right now.

"Don't move. Don't fucking move," I growl. Four of them are nursing broken bones, a leg, arm, nose, and wrist, while the one glaring at me is still cupping his balls.

"You think you're going to get away?" He smirks at me, and I find it comical he thinks he has a chance.

"I think you'll follow." I nod to the others. "They won't, but you will." I aim the gun at his foot. His eyes widen once he realizes my plan. He starts backing up, but I shoot. The bullet hits just above the top of his foot.

"Fuck!" he screams as he goes down.

I turn and take off, making sure to keep my head on a swivel. I can't move that fast, but I refuse to give up. Somewhere in the fight, my phone and airpods fell, but I don't care. I know I need to get home. I'm starting to feel the adrenaline wear off. All of the blows and kicks I took are becoming far more prevalent. The knife in my thigh stings, but the actual wound itself burns and seems to be radiating down my leg.

I'm slowing down more and more. My vision itself starts to blur, but I'm close. I can see the edge of the woods. That means I'm near my neighborhood street. I can stop at a house and ask for help. The idea that I've managed to walk in this condition and gotten this far gives me another burst of energy. My steps quicken a little bit, but it doesn't last as long as I hoped.

"Drake!" someone yells.

But I don't see who it is before I start falling forward. Everything goes completely dark before I even hit the ground.

Chapter Five

☪ Blade ☪

I glance at my phone and rub my head. I didn't get Drake's usual text this morning, but I have received two calls from Kody that I haven't answered. It's not like him to call me, though, and I'm contemplating calling him back. Especially since I've been feeling like something is off today.

I'm just reaching for my phone when it rings again. "Kody?" I answer quickly when I see his number for a third time.

"Fuck, Blade! About time! I called Racer. Drake got attacked!"

"What?" I'm on my feet and running for the door in less than a second. My door flies open just as I reach it.

"He was attacked!" Kody shouts. "He's holding a fucking gun!"

"Blade! Drake was attacked! Let's go!" Racer shouts at the same time Kody does.

"I'm coming!" I pound out of my office after Racer. Axel sees us and follows without question, as does Bear, Wraith, and Razor, all of my enforcers. "Where are you, Kody?"

"At the edge of the running trail!" Sirens. I hear sirens. "Fuck, Blade. The cops are coming! What do I do? I didn't call them!"

27

"Hide the gun, Kody!" *Fuck. Oh fuck!* They can't find him with the gun on him. "Not on you! Toss it as far you fucking can!"

"They're too close! They're going to see me!"

"Then put it down your underwear! Tuck it!"

"They'll see me! Blade, what the hell do I do!"

We all jump on our bikes. "Just sit tight! We're coming!" We rev our engines as I hang up and put my phone in my pocket. We peel out of our compound. With me in the lead, we race to the head of the running trail near their house. It's Drake's favorite place to run. We've both been on that trail. I've fucked him on that trail.

Running at speeds we have no business doing, we arrive on Kody's street in record time. I see a perimeter has already been set up, complete with a barricade, but I'm not letting that stop me. The closer we get, the better I can see the rookie cop trying to be tough narrow his gaze more and more.

We park in front of the barricade and cut our engines. We get off our bikes. "You're letting me through," I growl.

"No, sir. I'm not. I have orders."

I glare. "If you think you're stopping me, you need to think that through a little harder."

"Look. I have my order. No one through. This is a crime scene."

Without a second thought, Axel reaches out and has one arm around the kid's neck before he has any time to react. "It wasn't a request," he growls as he disarms the rookie in less than a second and hands me his gun while the guy fights the sleeper hold he's never getting out of. I take the gun with a smirk.

"Blade!" someone barks. I look up to see a sergeant who's one of my contacts. Bridger Jacobs.

"Better tell your boy his fucking orders don't apply to me," I growl as Axel lets him go.

"Back off, Richards!" Bridger yells at the rookie.

I duck under the police caution tape and hand the very shaken kid his gun back without saying a word as my crew follows me. I make my way quickly to where Bridger is with a trembling Kody and groaning Drake.

"Jesus Christ." I kneel down next to Drake and cup his cheek. He looks ashen and is bruised as fuck but leans into my hand. Racer kneels next to Kody, who's sitting in the dirt hugging his knees.

"Neither of them want to talk to me. They kept saying to get you," Bridger says as he kneels next to me and drops his voice low. "I can't take him in, man. He was stabbed in the leg. I removed the knife. I could tell it wasn't hitting any arteries or bone or anything. It went clean through the other side. The wound is on the outside of his leg."

I look down at his leg and see Bridger dressed it well. It's tight. "Kody, I need you to go get your car."

Kody stares blankly at me before I see him snap out of it and nod. He stands up quickly. "What about the other thing?" he asks, still shaky.

"Where is it?"

He points in the direction he threw the gun. "I panicked. I threw it. It's over there."

"I'll take care of it. Racer, get him to his house. Get the car. Follow him back here. Also, call the doc. Have him meet us at the compound."

"You got it." He takes off with Kody on his heels.

Drake groans a little bit, and I look down at him. "Gunshots... They killed... them..."

"What?"

Drake closes his eyes and grips my leg. "Parents..."

"Baby, I can't make sense of that. Who killed them? Killed who? Your parents?"

Drake groans in response, but tightens his grip. "Parents..."

I swipe a hand down my face and look up at my guys. "Follow the trail. Look for anyone who could've done this." Axel nods. Bear, Razor, and Wraith move to follow him as I stand and grab Axel's arm. "He had to have shot someone. He had a gun when Kody found him," I say low enough so only he can hear me. I don't want to be overheard by anyone else. Not right now.

Axel nods again and takes off. My guys follow him as I take a breath. "Watch him," I say to Bridger.

"I got him. I'll get him into the car when they get back."

I nod before walking through the brush in the direction Kody pointed. I keep my eyes peeled for the gun, but it's not easy. The brush is overgrown, so I have to rely completely on any kind of reflection glinting off the metal.

I'm searching for several minutes before Bridger joins me. "I don't know how to report this, man. I can't take him to the hospital. It's an automatic report. I can report he was stabbed, but I have to explain shit about suspects. What do you want me to do?"

"I'll get you a report, Bridger. You know me."

"What about in the meantime? What do I tell the other cops out there? They have to write reports, too."

"Let them. They go to Colt. I'll take care of the rest."

"If I put them in the system -"

I turn to him. "Bridger. No system." I look at him deadpan so he fully understands what I need him to do. "This is off the books. Completely. Drake had a gun when Kody found him. It means he disarmed someone and shot him. You need to wait for my guys to get back just like anything else I run with you. Understand me?"

"Yeah." He nods. "Yeah. I got it."

"I'll get Colton out here. He can run the scene with you and help you along with this. I know we haven't worked too much together, but you need to trust me more. I'm not going to let you get in trouble, and I protect what's mine. Did you guys get him out of here?"

"Yeah. He's on the way to your compound."

I take out my phone and text Colton to get here. "Take out your flashlight. Search the brush. We need to find the gun. Under no circumstances does it get admitted to evidence. Where's the knife?"

"In my pocket."

I put my phone away as he takes out his flashlight. I hold out my hand. He reaches for the knife and hands it to me while he starts shining the light on the ground. "This is targeted."

"I know. I knew it the second Kody started asking for you. Found it." He starts heading towards the gun, but I hold him back.

"No. I got it." I take out a riding glove from my pocket and use it to pick up the gun he's shining his flashlight on. "You didn't see this."

"I saw nothing."

I chuckle. "Good man." My phone chimes. I take it and look at it. "Colt's on the way."

"Thank fucking God."

I grin and shake my head. "You know God isn't helping on this. Does the Almighty asshole really help anyone? Or is it all for Himself?"

Bridger grins. "Not a believer?"

"Nope. Not that I'll condemn you if you are, though."

"Grew up Baptist."

"I grew up Catholic."

Bridger groans. "That explains it," he teases.

I laugh as I put the gun in my pocket after picking it up and examining it. "My parents think they're God's disciples. I took my leave long ago. Left my sister and hated that, but I kept in contact with her, and she came to me when she could. Not that I don't believe He exists. Just don't think the fucker is as good as he's made out to be."

"I'm sure there are millions who agree with you. What do you want me to do now, Blade?"

"Wait for my guys and Colt." I start heading back to the trail. Bridger follows. "Let Colt take control of the scene. I'm heading to my compound to be with Drake."

"What about his parents?"

"Kody's parents don't need to know anything. Not right now."

"What if they start asking questions?"

"Tell them the scene has nothing to do with their kids. Have them call Kody."

He takes a breath as we get back to the trail. "I'm sorry. This is all fucked up. The biggest thing I've been involved in with you."

"Trust. I have your back. There's Colt. I'm gonna take off."

"Thank fuck."

I laugh, noticing the intentional leaving out of God, and pat him on the shoulder as Colt strides towards us. I meet him halfway. "Xavier and the cousins are on the way to your compound."

"Okay. Good. My guys are on the hunt. I told them to come here when they found the people who attacked Drake. I know at least one of them was shot. Kody found Drake with a gun. He wouldn't have it if he hadn't needed to use it."

Colt raises an eyebrow. "He owns one?"

I shake my head. "No. But he knows how to disarm and shoot if needed. I taught him."

"Where's the gun?"

"I have it. I have the knife that was found in Drake's leg, too."

"Where's Drake and Kody? Compound already?"

"Compound, or at least on the way to it. I have our doctor looking at him. He'll be off the books."

"Good. I'll take care of the scene. Get reports for me and the Sergeant on scene. The others -"

"Axel put your rookie in a chokehold."

"Jesus Christ, Blade. Do you have to make my job fucking harder? Get the hell out of here." He smirks as he shakes his head.

I laugh as he walks around me. I head directly for my bike and jump on. As I'm heading back to the compound, my mind is racing. Kody said gunshots and parents. I have to figure that out, but that's not what's at the forefront of my mind.

I never should've thought pushing him away from me was the best decision. He got hurt because of me. Because of my stupid decision. In my effort to protect him, I could've lost him today because he was on his own with no protection. I'm never gonna forgive myself for this.

I don't deserve Drake in the slightest, but I need to get him back.

He's my entire world, and I royally fucked up.

If it means I have to grovel for his love for the rest of my life, I'll do it as long as it means he's by my side.

Chapter Six

☪ Drake ☪

(Two Days Later)

I turn over on my side with my back to Blade when he comes into his bedroom. I've barely talked to him at all since I came to. My injuries are very superficial, thankfully. I don't have any broken bones. The most painful thing is the wound from the knife, and not even that's too bad. The doctor stitched me up and gave me some good pain pills.

Blade's guys caught all of the guys who attacked me. They were all interrogated. Turns out, it was a hit. Come after me, get to Blade. I guess they didn't expect me to fight back. Their plan was to leave me for dead in the woods after beating the shit out of me. They intended to inflict enough injuries that I would've just bled out internally.

I guess it all goes back to a larger gang, the gang Blade has been worried about. The one he deemed a big enough threat to make a decision that almost cost me my life.

And that's where we are now. Him feeling an intense level of guilt, and me being pissed off that he thought I'd be better off without him and getting hurt because of it. I'm likely to be out the entire rest of the season. He knows football is an important part of my life.

Just like he is.

"I brought you some soup. Your favorite. Homemade chicken noodle." Blade's voice is low and filled with sadness. A sadness that hurts me, even though I'm so angry at him.

I say nothing. I haven't known what to say to him all this time. I don't know how to express that I don't want to be away from him, but I'm so fucking pissed. I don't know what I'm supposed to say.

So instead, I stay lying with my back to him. I feel like everything we've fought for, all we've been through, everything we've done to stay together has been for nothing. All of the talks we've had about us feel like just words.

I don't even know why I'm still here. I could've gone home with Kody. The problem is my home isn't with Kody. It's with Blade. My home is where he is. Maybe that's why it feels like my heart hurts even more than it should. Maybe that's why I'm holding onto this resentment. Maybe it's because I feel like I'm in limbo. Like I've lost my safety. My place of comfort.

I feel like I've lost him.

I'm afraid to let myself get close to him again because I don't want to feel like he's uprooting my entire life again. Like I'm sure he will when I'm better. When I won't need to rely on him for help. It still hurts to walk, and I actually need physical help sometimes.

"Maybe I'm better off with Kody," I murmur. I close my mouth. I hadn't intended to speak those words out loud.

Blade sighs. I hadn't felt him sit on the bed, but I feel him shift. "I'm so fucking sorry, Drake."

It's the hundredth time he's uttered those words. And for the hundredth time, I can't seem to speak. I can't tell him what he wants to hear because I don't know if I forgive him or not. All I know is that I can barely think clearly. I have so much shit running through my mind that I don't know how to articulate, and not all of it even has to do with him.

"Drake, come on, baby. Talk to me, please? Or don't. Just eat something. At least I know I'm doing something good for you, then. Something right."

His words sting my heart. I know how bad he feels about pushing me away. I know he thought it was the right decision. I know he realizes now it wasn't. It's not his fault that I don't know what to say or do right now. He doesn't know how broken I feel. That's not his fault either. I haven't told him.

I carefully turn over and pull myself up so I'm leaning against the headboard of his bed. He reaches for me to help, but hesitates. It's not his fault that one simple motion hurts me more. "You're not going to fucking break me," I grumble. My words cause him to jerk his hands back, and I realize he took them in a way I didn't mean.

He lets out a quiet breath and nods. He settles the lap table over my lap with the soup and a handful of Sour Cream and Onion chips. He knows I hate crackers with my soup. I like to drop a chip in the bowl and scoop it up with some of the soup. I do it with all kinds of soup.

"I don't really know what to say right now other than I'm really sorry. I fucked up."

I nod and eat like he told me to. Only, I do it in silence. I know how much that hurts him. I don't mean to, but I have to get my thoughts together. If I don't, neither one of us are going to be at peace. It's not like me to give him the silent treatment. I might hide my emotions well, but I've never been able to do that with him.

Once I finish the soup, I adjust myself so I'm sitting up more. I can't bring myself to look at Blade, but I take a deep breath. "I'm pissed, Blade. I'm pissed."

"I know. I deserve that."

"You've made so many promises to me over the past couple of years, and then turn around and push me away again when things get too hot, or we get too close. That's why I'm so pissed. I can't honestly sit here and say that what happened wouldn't have if we had been together because I don't know. It could've happened before practice or after. It could've happened on a run. It could've happened at any given moment. What hurts, though, is that *you* thought I'd be safer and better off without you. What the fuck else do I have to do to prove to you how in love with you I am? How I'm not whole without you?" I finally bring myself to look at him. "How am I supposed to trust that you feel the same if you think I'm better off without you? Shouldn't you feel the same for me as I do for you?"

35

He looks up from his lap, pain contorting his beautiful and rugged features. "I do, Drake. It's just different. It's different for me because I -"

"I've heard it before. You've never been so deeply in love, and it scares you. The idea of losing me scares you." I search his deep, nearly coal eyes. "Don't you understand that losing me doesn't just mean me dying? That it also means me not being in your life in any capacity? Is that what you want? Because that would be worse than death for me. Not having you at all would be worse for me than you dying. I don't want either of those things to happen, but I'd rather love you as hard as I can for as long as I'm allowed to then be apart from you. At least I can hold onto the memories. At least you'll know when you take your last breath that I loved you with all of me. Don't I deserve the same?"

Blade doesn't hesitate to lean over and kiss me. His hand grips the back of my neck, and he pulls me closer, pouring all of his passion and soul into the kiss. I close my eyes and let it heal all of the cracks and bruises. His tongue swipes over my lips, and I part them, giving him access to me. He shifts and pulls me closer to him, deepening the kiss impossibly more until we're both breathless.

When he pulls away, we're both panting. Somehow, I've managed to tangle myself around him. My fingers are tucked into the waistband of his jeans. He's holding me tight with one arm and still gripping the back of my neck with the other.

"I absolutely fucked up. It was a very stupid decision on my part. I thought I was doing the right thing, but I should have known better. History has proven time and time again that two people who love each other should never be apart. It's never the best option. I learned a very hard lesson, and I learned it well. I'm not walking away from you again, Drake." He leans in and kisses me softly. His words sink deeper and deeper into my soul, but this time, I know he means them. When he pulls away, his other arm wraps around me to pull me into a hug I had no idea that I needed. "I'm never trusting your safety to anyone other than me again, baby. I'm sorry I lost sight of everything. Of my love for you and how much I need you in my life. How deeply a part of me you are."

A lot of people wouldn't know it from just saying he'll never trust my protection to anyone else, but I know he's talking about God. He's never actually told me the reason behind why he has such a broken relationship with Him, but I've always gotten the feeling it has something to do with his Catholic upbringing and sexuality. I've never bothered to ask. I always figured he'd tell me, but maybe now is the time.

"Are you an Atheist?"

Blade chuckles into my neck and shakes his head. "No. I believe there's a God and Devil. I just don't believe God is as good as people believe. He's vengeful. Conceited. Hateful. I think the Bible is filled with lies, and I think those who read it and follow it all down to every last letter have interpreted it how they want to and found ways to back themselves up. I think those who claim to be Christians and who are religious are the most intolerable and insufferable of all people in the world, and they use God and the Bible to back them."

I'm quiet for a few moments before looking up at him. "But you've never condemned anyone for being a believer in God."

"That's not my place. In the end, everyone is going to face a judgment. Just depends on who they're going to take it from. I'd rather go down with my fellow man knowing I'm a good person at heart. In the end, the people around me are all that matters. How they believe isn't any of my business as long as they don't shove it down my throat like my parents did."

"I've always wondered about your parents."

"I don't talk about them because they aren't worth talking about. I came out as gay when I was in my teens. They kicked me out. I didn't have a job. I was young. I dropped out of school and landed my ass on the streets. I got tough real quick because my life was on the line a lot. I never stooped to drugs because I had to be on my game all of the time, and I had to be of clear mind for my sister. She was the only one I still had a relationship with. I never knew where the next threat to me was going to come from. Hell, I didn't even know where my next meal was coming from. I spent a lot of time in soup kitchens. I volunteered in them just as much as I used them. Eventually, Crasher, the leader of VV before me, found me. He saved my life. I was at my wits end. I'd given up. I learned to put my faith in myself and those who stuck by me. I learned fate was something I needed to take into my own hands. I failed at those two lessons when it came to you, and those are the two roots I stand on."

I lay my head on his chest; my ear over his heart. The steady rhythm calms me enough to put my own thoughts into something that makes sense. "My parents were killed, Blade. I'm sure of it. Before you got there, I heard two pops. I've thought about it over and over. I think you scared them when you showed up, but if you hadn't, I think I would've ended up with a bullet in my head, too."

Blade stiffens and holds me even tighter against him. "What makes you so sure?"

"I don't know. I didn't see anything. I was fighting to stay awake, but I heard the pops. The more and more I replay them, the more positive I am that they were gunshots and not the car starting on fire. I remember it exploded right afterwards. I remember you covering me. It's taken a while, but I remember everything from that day. I remembered a lot before, but now, it's like something in my mind broke. I remember it all."

Blade takes a deep breath and rests his chin on top of my head. He rubs his hand up and down my arm as we both fall silent. Finally, he kisses my head. "Get some rest. You need it."

I chuckle. "I feel like all I've been doing is sleeping. And being mad. I want to play football."

"Doc said it's likely you'll be good to go in a couple of weeks. We just need to keep you off it as much as we can until he takes the stitches out. Then, we can introduce some physical therapy stuff for strengthening and conditioning. And again, I'm -"

I quickly press my lips to his and cut him off. "I know, babe. I know."

We fall into silence again, but this time, it's comfortable. This time, everything is on the table. Nothing is between us.

It feels like a fresh beginning where nothing is standing in our way.

Chapter Seven

☪ Blade ☪

After hours of talking, Drake and I are back on solid ground, and I couldn't be happier about it if I tried to be. My world isn't right without him in it, and I regret deeply that I thought being apart was the best idea. No matter how many times I apologize, it's still never going to be enough.

Drake fell asleep hours ago, and while I've held him tight and been the most content I've been since I left him two weeks ago, I still couldn't get a wink of sleep. Something he said has been nagging at me, and I can't make sense of it.

He said his parents had been shot. He heard gunshots. Could it have been? I was too far away to hear that, especially over the roar of my engine, but I remember seeing something glint. It could've been the sun reflecting off a mirror or something, though. I can't be sure, but if Drake says it happened, I believe him.

I turn, careful not to wake Drake, and reach for my phone. I text Colton to see if he can swing by this morning to talk about all of this. I want to get to the bottom of this because we've always believed something a lot bigger was at play that day. It's just never been something we've been able to figure out. Maybe this will help.

Drake has remembered a lot more stuff, more than just the gunshots. It could be clues about where they were going that day. I'll take anything if it helps get to the bottom of what happened. If gunshots were involved, it proves suspicions that have been circulating for a while. Drake's parents were murdered that day. It's always been too suspicious to just be a hit and run. Especially since the truck that did it came back to the scene.

Another thing that never made sense to me is that they were never caught, even though the cops were right there as I was entering the town with the truck behind me. I never understood how they got away and why they were never found. I gave the plate number and everything, but that truck was never seen again. The people who owned it said it had been stolen. They were an older couple, and the truck's plate was customized, as I thought. The numbers were birth years of their kid and grandkid.

Still, too many questions unanswered.

Drake stirs and moves closer to me. His perfectly muscular ass presses against my cock, and I'm instantly hard for him. It's been way too long since I've been inside him, but I know I have to earn my way back to that level of intimacy.

That control doesn't at all stop the groan that escapes my throat. When he pushes against me again, though, all of my resolve nearly snaps. "Baby, I -"

"Fuck me, Blade," Drake rumbles sleepily.

"Jesus…" My dick feels like it might break in half if I don't let it out of my underwear. I hold him tighter with one arm and bury my face in his neck while I shove the underwear down.

Drake pushes his down just enough to give me access to him. "I need you, Blade. Inside me. Right now."

I kiss his neck a little rougher than I intend, but the moan I get from him spurs me on. "Patience, Dray," I growl. "You know I'll rip you apart if I go in without a lube." I hold two fingers up to his mouth. "Suck. Get 'em all wet for me, sweet boy."

Drake grips my wrist and slowly sucks my fingers into his mouth. Watching him push them in turns me on just as much as his tongue lapping at my fingers. His saliva soaks them. He pulls them out slowly, but I waste no time bringing them to his puckered hole and pushing them both in. I know how he likes it. I know when he's this hot, he needs it hard. Fast.

40

"Fuck…" He drags out the word on a groan as I spread him apart. "Oh fuck." He relaxes around my fingers as I thrust into him, grinding my dick against his ass. I start slow with hard motions, gradually quickening my pace, until he's panting and writhing. It's how I know he's ready for me.

I take my fingers out slowly, drawing out his pleasure. "I need you, baby," I rumble.

"Then take me. Fuck me. Fuck me like you can't get enough of me." He looks over his shoulder at me. His eyes are full of lust and a promise that I'm about to be taken to the highest peak I've ever been on. The words that fall from his lips are like crack to me. I get harder and harder.

I spit on my hand and grip my dick. I give myself a few strokes and feel my precome mixing with my saliva, soaking my cock. "I can't get enough of you. I'll never get enough." I push the tip of my dick into him.

"Yes…," he hisses. He reaches back and grips my ass as he turns his head.

I slowly let my hand slide to his cock as I thrust into him deeper and deeper, but slowly. Just enough to drive him crazy. Once I know he's about to slam back on me, forcing my dick as deeply as it'll go, I crash my lips to his as he does just that. I take his hard length in my hand.

I moan into the kiss, swiping my tongue over his lips and forcing myself into his mouth. I stroke his cock at the same pace I'm thrusting, getting faster and faster while he gets wilder and wilder. His fingers dig into my ass as he tries to deepen the kiss impossibly more.

But Drake is never going to get control in this bed. He knows he belongs to me just as much as the power. He thickens in my hand, and I growl as I thrust into him. "Don't you dare come."

"Fuck, Blade. I can't -"

"You can. And you damn well better. Or I'll fuck you again and again, filling your sexy ass while keeping you so close to the edge you go fucking insane." His eyes darken. If I didn't know him so well, I'd think he's about to challenge me, but it's a mistake he made before and won't ever make again.

Like a good boy, he removes his hand from my ass and brings it to the back of my neck. He pulls me into his lips again, but instead of letting his tongue wrestle mine again, I dominate the kiss as much as I do him. I jerk his thick and very full cock while his ass clenches and pulses around me, bringing me closer and closer to my release. His precome leaks from his dick, and I spread it all over him as I stroke him. The sloppy sound my hand makes is like an aphrodisiac that spirals straight to my cock, making it impossibly harder.

"Oh fuck, Blade. Please, baby. Fill me. Give me your come. You know how much I love being claimed by you."

My stomach clenches. My back feels like it's vibrating. I'm gonna fucking explode. "Jesus Christ, Dray. Keep talking like that, and you'll have me on my knees begging to fill your ass."

His eyes meet mine. "Claim me, Blade. Claim me. Fuck me like I'm yours and only yours." His voice trembles slightly, and I know exactly what he needs from me.

"You belong to me, got that?" I punctuate my words with thrusts as he nods. His eyes fill with more and more lust and get heavier. "And I'm only yours. Understand?" I stroke him harder until I'm sure he won't be able to hold back.

"Yes, sir," he rumbles. His ass pulses and clenches tighter and tighter around me until I can't hold back any longer.

"No one gets to touch you, Drake. No fucking one," I growl as I give him a last hard thrust. I come hard and deep inside him.

He spasms uncontrollably around me. "Fuck yes, Blade...," he moans through clenched teeth as he takes all I give like a greedy come slut. I groan into his neck as I kiss it then suck on his sensitive flesh, physically marking him as mine.

I stop stroking him as I come. Once I've emptied completely, I pull out slowly. He moans at the loss, but he knows what's coming. I shift and push him onto his back as I straddle him, pinning his legs under me. I lean down and take his cock in my mouth, sucking relentlessly. He bucks into me and slaps his hands onto the bed, gripping the sheets.

Drake isn't as big as I am, but he's still got length and girth. I love having his dick in my mouth, but what I love more is swallowing his come. I run a fingertip from his pucker to underneath his balls as I stroke him, twisting my hand around him as I suck.

"Mmm...," I rumble low as I grip his balls in my other hand and roll them in my palm. He knows the rumble is his permission to come, but

I'm not going to take my mouth off his dick for the seconds it will take me to tell him. I enjoy him way too much to waste those seconds.

"Blade! Yes! Fuck yes!" he shouts as he arches his hips off the bed and comes hard. His come shoots down my throat, and I swallow around him like he's my last meal.

Only, he's not my last. He's my favorite. One I could eat every single day. Morning, noon, and night.

I pop my mouth off his dick and lay next to him. He cuddles into me like it's the most natural thing in the world. I wrap my arms around him and hold him close. Drake loves to cuddle after sex, and I would never deny him what he needs.

"Who did you text earlier?" Drake asks me after a few moments of silence.

"Colt. I've been thinking about what you said about the gunshots. I want to sit down with him and go over everything. See if maybe we can put more pieces together."

He nods as he wraps his arm around my waist. "I'd like that. I've always felt unsettled about it."

"So have I, baby."

I reach for my phone a few minutes later when I hear it vibrate. Colton will meet us at the clubhouse in a couple of hours. Which means I have Drake all to myself for a little while.

I want to do all I can and pour as much love and strength as possible into him because I think when Colton gets here, Drake's carefully reconstructed world is going to crumble once more. The only difference between now and before is he has me.

And I'm not going to let him fall.

Chapter Eight

☪ Drake ☪

A couple of hours after Blade made me feel whole again, he leads me into the Viper's clubhouse with my hand in his.

"Maybe I should become a member. I could be a Prospect."

Blade chuckles low. "Baby, you already are. I just haven't given you your cut yet because I've been too busy trying to keep you away from this life."

"Well, I go where you go. So… Don't think you'll be keeping me away." I grin as he glances over his shoulder.

He shakes his head with a smirk of his own. "I knew the second I laid eyes on you that you'd be my downfall." He glances at Racer as he comes out of the kitchen. "Where's Colt?"

"Office. He brought Sloane, though. Said something big is going down. Brant's in there, too." Racer takes a long drink of Gatorade out of a sports bottle, keeping one eye on Blade.

Blade pauses before he turns down the hall to his office. "Huh. Wanna join?"

"I would like nothing more."

Blade nods. "Figured you'd say that." He squeezes my hand and leads me to his office with Racer following.

Once we enter, Sloane is on her feet with her arms wrapped around my shoulders. "Hey, Sloane," I say, hugging her and lifting her off the ground. I'm over six feet. I tower over her.

"I feel like I haven't seen you in forever," she says when I set her back down. "How are you feeling?" She gingerly touches my bruised face.

"Eh. Okay. Little sore. It's mostly the leg, but not even that's terrible."

"You were so lucky, Drake," she whispers, tears shining in her eyes.

"Hey, man. Feeling better?" Brant gives me a side hug with a grin.

I hug him back. "Yeah. I am. Pissed I can't practice with you guys right now, but Doc says I should be okay to start slow. Should be back in no time."

"Hope so. We already miss you." Brant shakes Blade's hand and gives him a bro hug before we all settle.

Other than what Blade told me, I don't really know what's going on or why Sloane is here with Brant. I'm grateful to see my cousin and his fiance, but it puts me on edge. Sloane is an investigative reporter. Whatever she's involved with that brings her here can't possibly be good.

"Before I say what I'm going to, I'm curious why you've brought Sloane," Blade says once we're all settled. "Not that I don't like seeing you." Blade flashes a million-watt smile that makes my insides combust.

Sloane blushes. "Well, the truth is, I don't know what I have yet, but I was running it by Colt when he told me he needed to head out to come here. We decided to tag along." She slides a folder across Blade's desk.

I'm in a chair next to him and lean over to see what it is. I furrow my brows. "Sex trafficking?" I look up at her.

"Specifically." She nods. "Not just human trafficking. This is absolutely sex trafficking. Women with specific sets of features and attributes, and it's going right through Piper Falls."

I look up at Blade in shock. He leans back in his chair and folds his arms over his broad chest. "How did you stumble across this?" His eyes meet Sloane's.

45

"I was in New York a little while ago and caught wind of a story someone was working on. It just kind of intrigued me, so I asked a few questions to the reporter working on the story. Turns out, she stumbled across a woman in New York who flashed her four fingers. She recognized it as code that something was wrong. She followed and called the police. She ended up getting a couple of guys to help her out, though, because the guy who was with the woman grew suspicious and started dragging her towards the subway. They got her away, and the police ended up taking down a small trafficking ring up there, but something just sort of made her keep digging. The woman talked to her some and said she was from San Antonio."

I glance at Blade before resting my elbows on his desk. "Wasn't there just a huge story on the news about a woman disappearing from San Antonio? Just vanishing?"

"Yep," Colt says. "She was seen here. We got a call from a concerned citizen. She looked dirty and ran into a bar for help. By the time squads got there, she'd been dragged out by someone. We got a description of a tall guy with dark hair. That was really all. No cameras in the area. No plate. We searched for the car, but witnesses gave us three different descriptions and were all very sure it was right. We had nothing to really go on, but we still kept searching the town. We even went door to door in the area. Nothing."

Blade leans forward and points to Colton before looking back down at the folder. "Wonder if you can't get info from New York about it. Maybe interview the reporter."

"The thing is," Brant interrupts, "that's not all Sloane found. This trafficking ring seemingly originates in Texas. She's trying to track down where, but this name keeps popping up. We wondered if maybe you'd heard of them."

Blade raises an eyebrow. "Who?"

"Santos Del Infierno," Slone says.

"Saints of Hell," I whisper. "That's a pretty big Latin gang." I look at Blade, knowing that he's already on the same page as me.

Blade sighs and rubs his head. "Sloane this is fucking huge. You have no idea what you've just stumbled on. You need to pause this investigation. It's way too dangerous."

46

Sloane clears her throat after a few moments of complete silence in the room. "What's… happening…?"

Colton lets out a breath. "They're who attacked Drake. Well, a very small part of them. They were just a group of kids fucking around, but Santos Del Infierno absorbed them."

Blade groans. "They weren't that big, but it gives Santos Del Infierno a foot inside this town. It became a fucking turf war, and I wanted to avoid that shit. I would've been just fine taking the fight to them."

"They kind of already took it to you by attacking Drake," Brant says.

I nod because he's right. "You were already talking about taking them out since they've moved into the same hideout those five kids had."

Blade looks at me a little sadly. "Yeah. I was. I already had an attack planned. The problem is if this is the case, if they're linked to trafficking, I have to go about this differently. I need to know where they're keeping the people they take for this ring. I need to know more about it. And if it's a larger operation that extends further than Texas, then we need to mobilize other chapters. We need to know where they are. What states."

I take a breath and slump a little. "I should've known it wouldn't be so easy."

Blade rubs my back soothingly before dropping his hand to my leg. "I don't want to take them out here in Texas only to have them come at us from other states. Or countries." He squeezes my thigh. I smile a little, but I'm not feeling at all confident at how big of an operation this is going to be.

Colton sighs. "What did you want to talk about, Blade? May as well just pile it on." He hugs Sloane. We all know her well enough to know she needs reassurance that she's not doing something wrong by adding more to anyone's plates. Her ex made her feel like that and way worse. She still struggles with it sometimes.

"It's about what Drake has been remembering from the day his parents were killed. And yeah. I used that word intentionally. They were killed."

Colton raises an eyebrow and looks at me. "What do you remember?"

"Yeah. What do you remember?" Brant echoes.

47

I chuckle dryly. "Gunshots. I remembered them in a dream the day of the attack. I've been obsessing over it, and I'm sure. Two shots."

"I looked at the autopsy report. It said the bodies were charred beyond recognition," Colton begins. "But there were things that were redacted in reports and the autopsy. I'll look into them more."

"I also remember where they were taking me," I say. "They were in jeans and t-shirts. Flannel. They only ever wore that shit when we were going riding. We always went out to this ranch a few miles out of town. Calvary Ranch."

"Calvary," Blade says. "Isn't that Jay Calvary? FBI, right?"

Colton is silent for a few moments before clearing his throat. "Calvary came in asking questions after that accident. That's when I started digging because no one was being too cooperative with him. Especially your dad's brothers."

"Well, we know why that was," Sloane grumbles. Brant puts an arm around her. She's right. His brothers were cops with Brystone Springs. Both of them went down for some corrupt and abusive bullshit and were fired from the department.

"You don't think they had anything to do with my parent's death," I state, staring deadpan at Colton.

"I don't know. Not sure I ever will, but I'm also not sure I wouldn't put it past them. Especially if they knew shit they shouldn't have." Colton narrows his eyes as he falls silent.

"I think the best thing to do is talk to that FBI agent. See what he knows, if anything," Blade says.

"Couldn't agree more." I start to stand, having every intention of going with him.

Blade puts a hand on my thigh. "You have shit to do at the school today," Blade says sternly.

I furrow my eyebrows. "No, I don't."

"Yes," he reiterates, his eyes taking on a pleading look. "You do."

I have no idea what he's talking about. It's Saturday, but it's obvious he doesn't want me tagging along with this. I glance at Brant. "Uh. You free today? Maybe we could go pick up Kody, Sterling, and X."

"Go, Brant. I have Sloane," Colton says, obviously picking up on something we're not. Brant looks just as confused as me.

48

"Okay. Yeah. Sure," Brant finally responds after we both stare at each other. "I think we can figure out something to do." He stands and leans down to kiss Sloane. "Be careful," he rumbles.

"What's going on?" I ask Blade.

"I need you to do something else, Drake. Trust me." He kisses me. I stand and follow Brant, still confused. "Racer, go with them. Take a few others."

"You got it, Prez." Racer grins at me, and I suddenly understand. I look back at Blade. "Be careful."

"Always."

Blade, Colton, and Sloane stay seated as Racer follows Brant and I out. Once we're outside and in Brant's car, he looks at me. "What the fuck was that about?"

"Blade is going to take Sloane's information on the trafficking. Then, he and Colton are going to take her while they do their own investigation."

"The fuck they are." Brant reaches for his door handle, but I stop him.

"Something he saw or something that was said makes him think my parents had information they shouldn't have. Whatever that information was, he wants us far away from it."

"So, he's going to let Sloane in on it and put her in danger? He's fucking insane. I'm not allowing that." He tries to open his door again, but I put my hand on his arm.

"Brant, she's a reporter. And come on. Do you honestly think anyone is getting near her with Colton and Blade around? You know damn well he'll have others with him. And you also know that he'll put protection on her. Whatever she found though Brant, puts her in danger. Fucking deep and dark."

He closes his eyes and leans his head back against the seat as he grips the steering wheel. After a few moments he opens his eyes and starts the car. "What the hell did she get into, Drake?"

"By the looks and sounds of it? Something far over her head, man. Whatever it is, I think I'm somehow involved in it, too. The only thing I can think of is that my parents knew something. I've been around Blade and his crew or ya'll ever since the accident. I'm not often alone. Ironic that the one time I choose to run without someone is the day I'm attacked, huh?"

"Fuck," Brant whispers as he heads to the road. Four bikers, including Racer, tail us. Brant glances in his rearview mirror. "He better keep her safe, Drake. Hell, he better keep you safe."

"All of us, man. All of us at this point."

We both don't say anything else as he drives towards Kody's house, but he's right. Whatever Blade figured out is a huge problem, and I have a very uneasy feeling about where it's going to lead. I think all of us are going to need each other more than ever before this is over.

Chapter Nine

☪ Blade ☪

I take the last drink of my coffee as I stare in disbelief at Jay. "So, you're saying you handed this over to Lucinio Mafia?"

"Crane, actually," Jay tells me. "The second I got kicked from it."

"Which was a week ago," Colton reiterates.

"Yep. Ryan has been a contact for a long time. The reason I didn't call him in earlier is because I was starting to make some headway. And that's when I got kicked. Ironically, when Senator Remington went down for treason is when I started to find more shit out and connect dots that hadn't been there before."

"And that's when your boss pulled the case?" Sloane asks, furiously writing in her notebook.

"Yep. Fucker wanted all my files. All the backups. Everything. But I printed everything I had. Two copies. One for my files, and one to hide. I had backups on flash drives. I gave him all of my electronic copies. He took my laptop, computer, phone. All of it. They even raided my house."

"Christ," I growl. "What did Crane say?"

"He hasn't checked in yet. I handed off the files to him last week, but we made a plan for him to come here to do that because I was being

51

watched. Probably still am, but he wanted it known to anyone watching that he's on this. The only reason I can even talk freely to you is because he put the mafia on me for protection."

I chuckle. "I saw a couple blacked out SUVs on my way in. I thought they were FBI."

"Nope," Jay drawls with a grin. "Dirty FBI agents think they can fuck with one of their own? Not a chance. Pretty sure they're running scared right now. They put me on a no-fly list, though. Guess I'm a national threat."

"Well, you sound pretty dangerous." Colton grins.

"So, what exactly did you find out?" Sloane asks. "Why are they running scared?"

Jay gives a lopsided grin. "This can't get out yet, sweetheart. You know that," he drawls, his Southern accent deep.

"Oh, I know. But Blade believes this all ties into the bigger picture of my story. Colton agrees. My goal with this is to take down a lot of bad guys I think are higher ups in many powerful organizations. I'm willing to sit on this until the perfect time as long as these people are taken out. I want people to be safe, and they won't be with this stuff happening."

Jay grins at me and Colton. "I like her. Okay. Here we go. Here's what I know for sure. Santos Del Infierno. Heard of 'em?"

"Yeah," we all say together.

"They aren't a national gang. They're just here in Texas, but they think they're a lot bigger than they are because they've managed to align with bigger and smaller Latin gangs. They're an ally to Latin Kings and encroaching on Hell's Angels and Blood territory all over this state."

Colton chuckles. "No way that's going over well. Both of those organizations could obliterate the entirety of Latin Kings, no matter how many people they align with."

I nod. "There's a reason I don't fuck around with Hell's Angels. We coexist. They leave us alone. We leave them alone. And if we need each other, we call. We're not exactly allies, but we're smart. I think Latin Kings are the same with the Blood's. Maybe not the calling each other part, but they coexist."

"No, you're right," Sloane chips in, chewing the tip of her pen. "I did a thesis paper on gangs. They really tend to stay out of each other's way unless their territory is being infiltrated. Not that that was the case

52

before, but new leaders are actually taking past actions and learning from them. It's why they're becoming more and more powerful, but their wars aren't making national news anymore."

I smile. "Which is why the smart thing to do to take them down is from the inside. This smaller gang that Santos Del Infierno absorbed was trying to impede on my territory. Which means that Infierno was intending to expand into territory not theirs. You said they're aligned with Latin Kings?"

"Yep," Jay confirms.

"Then time for Latin Kings to take them down," I shrug.

"Well, before you do that, there's more," Jay begins. "What got me removed from the case is that I stumbled upon a sex trafficking ring that Senator Remington was involved in. So were two of his brothers that I could confirm. Buckley Remington and Remy Remington."

We all freeze and look at Sloane. She focuses on her notes. "One more thing to add to his list of transgressions against the human race," she mumbles.

I look back at Jay but keep glancing at Sloane. "Uh… what about the accident? What do you know about that? Drake remembered they were on their way here to your ranch the day of the accident."

"Yeah. They were. That was something that wasn't in the reports. Drake was interviewed and couldn't remember. I've talked to him a couple of times, and that never changed. He didn't remember, but he did say that they were taking him somewhere to surprise him. He just didn't know where. When did he remember?" Jay asks.

"After he was attacked," I confirm. "He also remembers two gunshots." I leave it there, hoping he'll give us something.

Jay whistles between his teeth. "I had suspicions. The autopsy report didn't make sense to me."

"Me either," Colton agrees. "Fire got there quickly. Their report said the car was on fire, but not engulfed. They mentioned the gas tank and the engine. Paramedics said when they got there, FD already had the fire almost out. Police reports had a lot of redacted shit I couldn't see."

"Shit like the bodies were unrecognizable?" Jay asks.

"Yeah, but if we go by fire and medical, the cause of death would've been smoke inhalation. Not even they mentioned bullet holes, though."

"Not sure they would've seen them," I say. "There would've been a lot of blood anyway just from the accident. I bet the cops took over pretty damn quick."

"So, wait," Sloane interjects. "Why were you involved?"

"Good question," Jay says. "The answer is because Drake is right. They were coming here. Decker and Gladys said they had something to discuss with me. They didn't tell me what, but they said they discovered something they didn't know what to do about. The very next day was the accident. I had a lot of suspicions."

"I think we all did," I say. "Colt and I were discussing how it seems odd that truck was never found, and neither were the drivers. Even more strange they took off when I was pulling up, and then came back. Why not stay away? Why come back and chase me knowing I'd probably called for help?"

"Did Drake recognize them?" Jay asks hopefully. "Because I have suspicions. Even some evidence to back it up. I just can't prove it. Everything is circumstantial."

"He just said he saw the eyes. They were cold. Almost demonic. They were both wearing handkerchiefs over their faces, which checks out. That's what I saw when they came back." I rub my temples. "Fuck, this is fucked up."

"I have a feeling it's only going to get worse," Sloane says. "You said you could confirm this gang is involved in sex trafficking? Because my research so far calls them out."

"I know they're involved in at least one case." He hands Colton a folder. "I made another copy of everything I gave Ryan. What's in that folder is the other copy. I have one more copy hidden in a safe place. Just in case. Maybe you can help put everything together. I have a few dots connected, but there's a lot of other shit in there that I see very clearly but have nothing more than intuition to go on."

Colton takes the folder and hands it to me. "Blade and I will look it over. He'll keep it with him. He can protect it a lot better than I can."

Jay nods. "Yeah. I agree. One more thing." He looks at Sloane. "I don't think you should be alone."

"She won't be," I tell him. "I'll have protection on her."

Sloane nods. "That was already decided before we even left Viper's Venom's property."

"Good. Because the shit in that folder is a game changer. I have some very powerful people after me because of it. I think if everything I found turns out to lead to where I think it will, a lot of people and powerful operations are going down." Jay stands. Colton, Sloane, and I follow his lead. "Take care and watch your backs. And each other's." He reaches out to shake our hands.

"Will do," I say as I shake his hand. Colton follows. Sloane is last. I can tell she's shaken over this. We all walk out of his house in silence, our heads on a swivel as we pile into Colton's truck. It's not until he's driving that I start breathing. "Sloane and the cousins stay with me. You, too, Colt," I finally say.

"I was going to suggest that," Sloane whispers from the backseat.

"So was I," Colton agrees. "This is bigger than me." He glances at me before focusing back on the road.

"Which is why you're not touching it," I tell him.

He only nods. It's the first case he's ever had that he's turned over to me. It's good that he recognizes the level of danger here. I take out my phone and dial a number I never thought I'd have to ever call.

"Yeah," a growly voice answers.

Juan Collazo.

Leader of the Latin Kings.

"Mr. Collazo. It's Blade. President of Viper's Venom." I portray power. Control. Confidence.

He chuckles. "Blade. What can I do you for?" His accent is thick. It sounds like I'm speaking to someone from across the border. Juan, however, was born and raised right here in the good 'ole US of A.

"I got some trouble in my neck of the woods. Nothin' I can't handle, but I got some information here that's going to piss you the fuck off."

"Hmm... and what's that, Mr. Prez? Got some trouble with one of my allies?" Fucker is grinning. I don't need to see it. I can hear it in the taunt he's projecting.

I grin. He has another thing coming if he thinks he's going to get one over on me. "You mean Santos Del Infierno? Nah. I can't take care of them."

"Well, you don't wanna be bringing peligro to your doorstep, do you? Go after mi amigos, you have to deal with me."

"I don't want that," I drawl. "But I'd check to see if they're really your amigos."

There's a long pause, and I grin at the seed I've planted. Finally, Juan speaks. "What do you know?" he growls.

"Your amigos ain't who you think they are, buddy. From what I gathered, they want Texas. They're telling everyone that you're coming after us all. Pissing a lot of us off. I don't think you want us all banding together, do you? Imagine it. Hell's Angels, Bloods, Viper's Venom. All teamed up."

He swallows hard as he thinks. Another few moments of silence later, he takes a breath. "Look. I'll take care of it. Confia en mi."

"I don't trust anyone, Juan. You know better than that. Fix it. Or my next call is to the Bloods and Hell's Angels." I hang up the phone before he has a chance to respond.

"You sure that was a good idea?" Colton asks.

"Yep. He'll come to me for help. He'll give me all of the information I need. And to protect myself, I'll go in there with both Hell's Angels and the Bloods."

"That sounds like a terrible idea," Sloane says softly.

I chuckle. "It's not the first time I've teamed up, sweetheart. It won't be the last."

What I don't say is that my ears will be to the ground. Any kind of mumbling from Latin Kings or Santos Del Infierno, I'll know. And while all of this is going on, I'll be doing my research. If these fuckers are involved in trafficking, I need to know because I have to prepare for the fallout. It's likely if there's a trafficking ring, it will involve Hell's Angels and the Bloods, but having them involved in the takedown I'm planning will show good faith on my part. Protecting their turf even though I have a whole other game going.

I text Ace, the President of our entire organization. There's no way this isn't about to get bloody. I need everyone on this.

Chapter Ten

☪ Drake ☪

"So, he just said you need to do something else? Doesn't sound like him," Xavier says. We're all gathered at Kody's house, me, Kody, Sterling, Brant, and Xavier.

"Yep. We took off, but we think Sloane really opened the door to something," I tell him.

"I'm fucking nervous," Brant says. "I know what Sloane stumbled on, and I really think she needs 'round the clock protection."

"What did she stumble on? Did she tell Colt?" Xavier asks.

"Yeah. And Blade. It's a sex trafficking ring. Some gang that Blade and Colt are already aware of are involved somehow. This girl in New York already published her part of the story. They caught a couple of people, but she didn't give a lot of detail in her story. Sloane dug deeper. She's like a dog with a bone on this. I've begged her to stay off it, but she won't. I finally got her to go to Colt, at least, but Blade texted Colt this morning. Colt knew this was bigger, and he'd have to bring it to Blade. Turns out the cases both are working to connect."

"At least, that's what we think they're thinking," I finish.

"This is a lot." Sterling rubs his head. "I mean, if your parents were taking you out to an FBI agent's ranch, maybe they really did know something. They didn't hint?"

I shake my head. "Nope. Nothing. They were happy that day. They didn't seem to have a care in the world. They didn't seem worried about anything before that either. They didn't seem stressed or worried in the days leading up to the day they were killed."

"I find it pretty fucking interesting that both my dad and X's go down for some crazy bullshit not long after Drake's parents are killed. It feels like it's connected somehow." Brant stands and starts pacing Kody's bedroom. "And then Dylan's dad goes down for treason? That's four of our dad's down now. It's like a damn epidemic with the Remington family."

Kody lays back on his bed with a groan. "Makes you question everything, huh? Who's good? Who ain't?"

"Yeah." I look down at my phone. "I think I'm gonna Facetime Dylan."

"Probably a good idea. Maybe her boyfriend can help out," Sterling says. "Besides, if this is a trafficking issue, it could get pretty fucked up quick, right? Maybe we should be preemptive and get help right off."

I nod and start calling her. She picks up with a huge smile. "Hey, Drake! Miss you!"

I grin. She's wearing a bikini, and it looks like she just got out of the water. "Having fun?"

"Oh my God, yes! We're lake tubing and water skiing. It's a blast!"

Another face comes onto the screen with a huge grin. "Hey, guys. What's up?"

"Cole. Just the guy we needed to talk to." I turn my phone so everyone can wave.

"Uh oh. What do you need from me?" He puts his arm around Dylan so we can see them both. My cousins gather around me.

"We think we have a pretty bad situation down here," Brant begins. "Sloane stumbled on some shit when she was in New York. Turns out it's a sex trafficking ring involving the same gang that went after Drake."

"Actually, I talked to Josh after you guys called to tell me about that," Dylan says. "Turns out Ryan is already investigating something down there. Something about a FBI agent who found out some information after Foster went down for treason. Trafficking is involved."

I lean back in the chair I'm sitting in. "You know, it's interesting you say that because I remembered some huge details from the accident. One is two gunshots. I'm sure my parents were shot. Another is what they were wearing and where we were going. They were wearing riding clothes. We were going to a ranch owned by a FBI agent to ride. Blade's going out there with Colt and Sloane to talk to him."

"What's the agent's name?" Cole asks.

"Jay Calvary."

He nods. "That's who Ryan is working with. I'd sit tight. See what comes out of that, but I'll touch base with him and tell him what you remembered. I'll tell him about Sloane, too, and make sure he's aware of everything. In the meantime, what's Blade say?"

"I don't know, man. He sent me and Brant away. Basically told us to find something else to do. Obviously wanted to keep us away. Pretty sure he knew we'd gather the cousins."

"That's a good idea," Dylan says. "Strength in family. I think it's best to stick together."

"Well, I feel better knowing you guys are involved," Sterling says. "This sounds fucking huge to me."

"Trafficking is a big thing. You're close to the border. It's likely the cartel is involved. Best to make sure you have the big guns behind you," Cole agrees.

"Make sure you all talk to Blade. I'm sure he has a plan, but I really think maybe it's best in this case to stay with him?" Dylan furrows her brows in concern.

"That's actually not a bad idea," Kody agrees. "My parents are away for a business trip. I was gonna stay with X."

"I think she's right," Cole says. "I think until we know what's going on, stay with Blade at the compound. All of you. Even Colt. It sounds like shit is about to hit the fan, so it's a damn good thing Ryan is already on it. I'm sure Blade will be in contact with him. In the meantime, I'd pack some shit up. Stay together. Go to one house after another all together, then head to the compound together. It honestly just sounds like things are getting more intense."

"How are you feeling, Drake?" Dylan asks a little sadly.

"I'm good, sweetheart. Really. My leg hurts a bit, but everything is healing. I get to start working out with the team next week, even though it'll be slow. I'll probably miss quite a bit of the season."

"Well, I'll take that. I'm just glad you're okay." Dylan smiles softly. I know how worried she is, especially given she's not here. We've tried to make her feel close, though, by staying in contact with her and keeping her updated on everything going on with us.

After we all say our love yous and goodbyes, we hang up. Kody and I start packing some stuff. I don't know how long this is going to go on, but I've made a decision. Blade and I aren't going to be apart anymore. We belong together. No more pushing me away when he thinks things are too dangerous for me to be near him. This entire situation has proven to me that way of thinking doesn't work.

We stop at Xavier's and Colton's penthouse last and are surprised to see Blade already there with Colton and Sloane. Colton wraps his arms around Xavier the second he's within arms reach. They both start packing stuff.

Brant wraps his arms around Sloane and hugs her tight whispering something I can't hear in her ear. Once Brant and Sloane became an item, we all decided the house we were living in should become theirs. Kody and I moved back in with his parents. Sterling moved back in with his parents. We're all happy for them and for Xavier and Colton. They've found their one.

I smile when Blade wraps his arms around me. I melt into his embrace. "We decided we're all staying on the compound, but I guess you already decided that," I mumble into his chest as I hug him tight.

"I was about to call you. Colt was packing some stuff for him and Xavier. We were heading to Sloane's and Brant's next."

"We already stopped there. Brant got all of her necessities and enough stuff to last a couple weeks. I don't know where everyone's going to stay, but we called Dylan. Cole said he thinks this is about to blow up, and we should all be together."

"I have a couple guest houses. I don't think it'll be an issue. They can figure out who wants to stay where, but we found out more stuff.

Agent Calvary was working on your case. He hit a lot of dead ends until Foster Remington went down. He gave me the folder with all of the information he's found. Dots he's been able to connect. One of the biggest things is he said that your parents were going to him with information, but he didn't know what. I think I have an idea. I'm hoping what he gave me proves it. Colt agrees with me."

I look up at him. "What are you thinking?"

"Well, I think it has to do with the trafficking. I think he figured something out. Colt has some stuff from your mom's office he was telling me about on the way back here. He has it here. He's gonna grab it. One of the biggest things, though, is this trafficking. We know Santos Del Infierno is behind it. I planted a seed in Latin Kings about them wanting to take over territory from me, Hell's Angels, and the Bloods. Then, I called Hell's Angels and the Bloods about it all. They don't trust Latin Kings at all. So, they're teaming up with me. I thought this trafficking would somehow affect them, but they both shocked me. They brought it up first and said they aren't going down for shit they aren't involved with. They think Latin Kings are trying to frame them."

"So…, they want to team up to take out Santos Del Infierno… And they want to take out Latin Kings for this trafficking shit?"

"They think Santos Del Infierno is setting them up with the Latin Kings. They don't trust Latin Kings to take care of the problem at all."

I nod, understanding. "As long as this shit ends."

Once Colton and Xavier have all of their stuff, we all pile into our vehicles and follow Colton and Blade back to Viper's Venom's compound. To many, this is the most dangerous place in the entire state, but to us?

There's no place safer.

Chapter Eleven

☪ Blade ☪

(One Week Later)

"I think if the media ever realized the three of us came together to deal with this, the world would implode," Dean Rivers, President of the Texas chapter of Hell's Angels says.

Levi Waller, leader of the Blood, chuckles. "Probably, but these fuckers have this coming. And Latin Kings better keep their asses in line after this."

I rub the crick in my neck I have from laying on the fucking ground with my eyes focused through a scope on my AR-15. "They better. If I have to go after Latin Kings after this, I'm gonna be pissed."

"You and me both, man," Dean says. "I'll team up with you any day if it means clearing my name with this trafficking bullshit. We may not be on the up and up, but some of us have fucking morals."

"Dude, didn't one of your guys get caught up in Minnesota in a trafficking thing?" Levi asks.

I chuckle. "I think that guy just ran rogue."

"Nah," Dean says. "He knew what he was doing. There's a lot of chapters that do shit like that. But our new organization Prez is cleaning things up. Most of us are pretty peaceful now. Not to say fuck with us. That's still a mistake. We're just run a little differently now."

"Yeah, we're still wrapped up in some illegal shit, but trafficking ain't one of 'em." Levi growls a little as he settles himself behind his gun, an AK-47 I'm sure came off an illegal shipment. "Still think it's funny the three of us are teamed up on this, though."

"The three of us own Texas, man. When we team up, people need to watch out." Dean sighs as he looks over his scope. "Is it time yet?"

"Still waiting on one more person," I say, looking at my watch. "Should be here by now, though."

"Think someone tipped him off?" Levi glances at me.

I shake my head. "I don't think anyone would dare. Juan is running scared right now. The story that broke in New York led the FBI down here. They're looking for any kind of clue the ring runs through any of us. Hells Angels, Viper's Venom, Bloods, the Cartel, even Latin Kings. Juan knows damn well we're together on this and will turn on him in a second. He was all for us taking these guys out. Saves him the work. We're bigger anyway."

"Don't explain why he's absorbing these smaller gangs. What's his play?" Dean looks at me.

Levi answers. "I think that's simple. They want to expand. I think they think since they're right on the border, they should have the larger faction. They've been coming at me for a while."

I grin. "Maybe we should make it known you're allies with both me and Dean."

Dean laughs. "Good way to get them out of here for good."

"Right. After a bloody battle," Levi says. "Not a bad idea, though."

"Seriously, though. The problem is I don't think these guys are the end of the line. I think it ends with Juan."

Levi nods. "Me too." He points to a car pulling up. "Is that our guy?"

I look through the scope of my gun and smile. "Yep. Wait 'til he's inside, then we move in."

"Not me throwing in my two cents, Levi, but I'm with the Viper on this one about Juan," a voice comes over our earpieces. "I'm sick of the

Kings. They need to be taught a lesson. No matter how big they get, they can't beat us if we're with them and Hell's Angels."

"Not that easy, dude. Alliances take time and trust. Focus on this. We'll talk about all that later. We have a mission," Levi answers.

"You sure everyone is here, Blade?" Racer asks.

"All of the intel we have says these guys are small. Thirty-two. Full team meeting tonight, and we've counted thirty-two," I respond.

"Everyone clear on their assignments?" Dean asks.

"All clear," a chorus of voices says.

We're all outside Santos Del Infierno's hideout on the outskirts of Brystone Springs. We've had people here for the past week watching everyone coming and going. We know everyone is in the house now because we've been closely paying attention to everyone. The takedown is going to be simple, but we know they have weapons. They just aren't as high caliber as ours.

Just so everyone knows who we are and who the targets are, we've all made the decision to dress in black tactical gear. We all have body armor and headgear. When we go in, they'll think we're some Black Ops from the fucking CIA or something. They're not going to know what hit them, and that's the point.

We've decided when we round up and question everyone, we'll do it right here. It's a mutual location for all of us that all of our teams are in control of. No one has any one advantage over the other.

Except me, but that's not something I've mentioned to anyone.

I have Ace here with other guys controlling the perimeter. If anything at all goes wrong, and I need them to move in, my code phrase is *Eagle One. Fox Three.* It's a line from one of my favorite movies, *Independence Day.* If I say that, shit is about to get real.

"All teams. On my go," I say, my voice deepening as I switch to dangerous biker leader. I can feel the switch of the two men next to me, too. Everyone is suddenly extremely on alert and just as terrifying as I am.

Our goal is to send a message of unity. Latin Kings said this shit had been dealt with, but I don't think they realize just who they're fucking around with. There's a reason we have the reputations we do. A reason even the Government of this nation fears this alliance. Once this gets out, that we've come together and taken down the very small gang of Santos

Del Infierno, Latin Kings will know exactly what will happen to them if they cross us.

But it's not just them we're sending this message to. We're sending it to the trafficking ring that's running down here. We've already discovered it's not the cartel, though they have one of their own. One we're always working diligently to stop. We know Latin Kings are involved in it, but they aren't the head of it. It's run by someone else.

I take one more look around. "Go," I command.

I don't work much with outside groups because I never know how they're going to work with me and my rules, but somehow, everything comes together. We move in as a group, bust in the entrances simultaneously, and all have our weapons raised and pointed at heads.

"Everyone down!" I shout. "Now! Now! Move! On the ground! On the ground!"

There are several more shouts and commands for them to get down. Most obey. Some panic and run, but they end up in the arms of someone else on our team. The more brave ones start reaching for guns but end up with the butt of a gun against their heads.

"Run! Everyone run!" someone barks. I look up to see the kid I've learned is the leader of this bullshit. He's sprinting out the backdoor, but I know he's not getting far, so I walk casually after him as the others in the house take down the assholes in here.

Once I reach the backdoor, Racer already has the kid on the ground with a gun pointed to the back of his head. "Move. I fucking dare you," Racer growls.

"Yes. Please. Do it," I growl.

"Get off me!" the kid screams.

"No," Racer says, pushing his face down into the ground harder.

The shouts from inside are quickly dying down, and looking at the leader, I become sick. This gang is filled with kids. None of these guys can be older than twenty.

"You've gotta be fucking kidding me. How old are you?" I rumble.

"None of your goddamn business!" The kid, definitely of Mexican descent, spits at my feet.

I shake my head and kneel next to him. "You do know who I am, right?" I look up at Dean and Levi as they join me outside. The four of us take off our helmets, revealing our faces.

"I don't care who you are!" the kid screams.

Dean kneels next to me. "You sure about that?"

The kid glares at us, his eyes flicking and focusing on me. "You're the boyfriend of the kid I was supposed to kill. Got me in trouble for failing, and that asshole fucked up the guys I assigned to the mission. Broke a foot, a knee, a wrist, a nose, and fucking shot a guy."

I chuckle as Racer outright laughs. Levi grins. "Well, damn. You didn't tell me your boyfriend was such a fucking badass."

I shrug. "Well, you know. He keeps me on my toes." I look back down at the kid. "Manuel Rodriguez," I say. "See, I don't need you to tell me. I know every name of every person you have in that house. And none of you are getting out of this alive. I promise. Especially you for thinking it would be fun to take down Drake. What I *do* want to know, and you *are* going to tell me, is why the fuck go after him?"

"Oh, good question," Dean says with a grin. "You should probably answer it, too. I'm the leader of one of the most feared biker gangs in the entire fucking world, and not even I'm crazy enough to take on this fucker."

"Guess you ain't as bad as everyone says, then," Manuel says with a smirk. Racer gives him a face full of dirt for his trouble, and Levi shoots his foot. "Ah! Fuck! Fuck! You shot me! You fucking shot me!" He shouts and wiggles, sputtering and choking on the dirt.

"Now you match the other kid who thought he could be a badass," Levi says with a shrug.

"Maybe you should answer questions," I say calmly. "Because Levi is fucking crazy. He's pretty handy to have around, though. He's just a little trigger happy and has zero patience. Wanna try again?"

"Anonymous! It was… Anonymous! Ah! Get me a doctor!"

"Nah. You won't need one," Levi says. "Let's talk about this trafficking shit. I heard some shit about me and Dean being pulled into that. Even some rumblings about Blade."

"I didn't start that! I didn't, man! I swear!"

Levi chuckles. "I'm just gonna go ahead and keep shooting from your foot up. Kneecap next." He shoots again, hitting the back of Manuel's kneecap, eliciting another scream that pierces the otherwise quiet night. "Wanna try the truth this time?" Levi shouts above the loud shrieking.

"I fucking swear it! It was the same guy who sent us after that kid and his parents!" Manuel screams. He's crying now. Ugly tears with snot dripping into the dirt.

I pause. "Explain. Now," I command low and dominantly. Every bone in my body wants to beat it out of him.

"We were paid to do it, okay? We stole a truck. We ran head on into them. We shot them. We went to shoot the kid, but you showed up! We got scared and took off, but realized you were alone. We thought we could take you out with the kid, but you took off. We thought we were done for when the cops showed up, but after you went towards town, the cops backed off. Remington was our contact with them."

Levi looks at me. "Remington. As in Remy? That cop who had all those fucking accolades for gang takedowns?"

"Which Remington?" I growl.

"That one. Remy. But Buckley was involved. He's the one who took care of the truck." Manuel groans through gritted teeth. "I'm fucking bleeding out. Come on, man. I'll tell you whatever you want if I know the answer. Get some help for me, man!"

"You're still talking just fine," Racer says with a shrug. "Can't hurt that bad."

"Fuck," Manuel whimpers.

"You think that's who's pulling the strings?" Levi asks.

I shake my head. "Nah. Both of them were killed behind bars. Prisoners aren't so kind to cops, and the warden didn't grant either of them isolation. I paid him off. They were with the regular prison population."

Racer looks at me. "You think he even knows who this fucker is?"

I shake my head. "Nope. But I bet you his phone can give us some good information."

Dean stands. "I'll have the guys grab everyone's phones. We'll take 'em with us." He pauses and looks at me. "You still work with the mafia? They can probably get to the bottom of that shit quicker than any of us can."

I nod. "Yeah. I'll take 'em."

"Share the info," Levi says, looking down at me.

"Absolutely." I stand as Dean goes into the house. "Let's get him up and in the house."

Racer stands and pulls a whimpering and blubbering mess up with him. Levi puts his gun away and helps Racer get Manuel into the house. Once we reach the room where the rest of the guys are cuffed and on the floor, Levi and Racer shove Manuel roughly to the ground to join them. Levi cuffs him.

"Anyone get any more info?" Levi asks.

"A couple of them squealed like little pigs," one of our guys says.

"What did he say? Who?" I ask.

The guy points. "That one."

I look down at the guy. "Repeat," is all I need to say.

He looks up at me with wide eyes. "We get orders from a guy. No one knows who he is. We've never seen him!"

I sigh. "Okay. What else?" I cross my arms over my chest.

"We know the guy is from a rich family. Based somewhere in Texas. They're influential, but we don't know who the guy is or what family he's from. He threatened us a lot and used his family. That's all we know." The guy looks so dejected. I don't think he's any older than sixteen, and he looks fucking scared.

Dean growls low and looks at me. "I say we let the police handle this bullshit," he says low enough for only me and Levi to hear. "They're kids."

"Agreed," Levi says. "Not even I'm that heartless."

I nod. "I'll give it to a contact. Huge bust for him. We'll make him a hero cop. Clear your guys out." I turn back to everyone here. "Nobody moves. Anyone walks out of this house, you end up like your buddy here." I point to Manuel, who's still whimpering on the ground.

We start moving our men out, but we all stay in the shadows. Someone hands me their phones. To their credit, not a soul in the house even attempts to leave. As soon as Colton arrives on scene, we all leave. When I'm inside my SUV, I take out my earpiece and shut it off.

Racer follows. "That went way too smoothly."

"There's absolutely no way they're able to run a whole sex trafficking operation. Not a single one of them is older than the age of twenty." I call Ace and put the phone on speaker as Racer starts driving.

"Looks good. They're hauling them out now," Ace answers.

"I have the phones. Can you come by and collect them for Lance or Robby?"

"Yeah. I'll be there as soon as things are clear."

"Did you hear all the shit about this prominent family?" I ask.

"Yeah, there's a lot of them. We're gonna have to narrow it down, but we know for sure now that there was a hit put on Drake."

"What do I do, Ace? I can't let him out of my fucking sight."

"That's exactly what you do. He stays with you. You put protection on him, and we figure out just what the hell his parents knew."

"Ryan did call this morning. He thinks they confirmed this trafficking ring, and it is going right through the center of town. Calvary found that not only does it go through town, but two cops were involved and Senator Remington. Ryan confirmed that, too."

"Let me guess. Buckley and Remy."

"Correct."

"So, they found out his brothers were really fucking dirty, but before they could expose them, they were killed by those same brothers. At least that's what I got from what that kid said in there about Buckley and Remy. I bet they were the cops that showed up and backed off, letting them get away."

"Yeah, I haven't broke that news to Drake or any of the cousins yet, but it's what I think too."

"Shit, you better make sure Cole is around for Dylan when you break that to her. She still holds a lot of guilt about what that Foster fucker did up here. I don't know how she'll take the rest of this."

"Yeah, I thought we'd go up there for Christmas. Maybe we can break that to her then. That way they'll all be around for her."

"I don't know. That's still a bit of time away, but I'd still come up for Christmas and let them all deal with it and work it out after you tell them all." Ace pauses. "Cops are clearing out, Blade. I'll meet you at the compound."

"Thanks, man." I hang up as we're pulling into the compound. Racer parks at the clubhouse, and I beeline for my house.

I want to be the one to tell Drake everything we know, and I want it to be just us. Things will finally come full circle for him, and the mystery of his parent's death will be put to rest.

But it's going to be painful, and I want him in my arms where he belongs so he can feel safe while he lets everything go.

Chapter Twelve

☾★ Drake ☾★

(Two Weeks Later)

I toss the football to Xavier with a huge grin. It's my third practice with my team, and I'm feeling stronger and stronger. My bruises have almost completely healed, but I still get twinges of pain in my leg where I was stabbed. I reach down to rub the area as all of my teammates cheer.

"That was the best run you've had yet!" Xavier says once he reaches me. He pats me on the back but notices me rubbing my leg. "You okay?"

"Yeah. Just pushed too hard, but it feels good to be out here. I need this."

"Take this next drive out, Drake. We'll have the medical team check out your leg," Coach Steele says as he signals to our towel boy to grab me water and a towel. "Kody, get him to the bench."

Kody growls under his breath and glares at Coach Steele, but helps me to the bench. When we sit down, he shakes his head. "Remind me again why the fuck I still do this."

I grin. "I don't know. Because you love the game?"

"Enough to put up with a dick of a coach?"

I glance at the coach then back to Kody as the medical team checks out my leg. "What he do this time?"

Kody looks at me with his face screwed into disdain. "He just effectively took me out of this drive, dude. Without even saying it."

"Maybe he's making sure everyone has practice on the play."

Kody shakes his head. "No. We have a tough game coming up. He shouldn't be putting Hatford in like this. Hatford can't block worth shit. He knows that."

"Well, a good coach sees the weakness and tries to turn it into a strength."

Kody just grumbles and takes a drink of his water. "Sure."

I'm about to ask him what his problem is with our coach, but the trainer interrupts me. " I think we should go ahead and call it a day, Remington," he says. "You got a lot more practice in, but I'd like you to work more on the strengthening exercises we were talking about. Your muscles are still not where I want them."

"Whatever to get me out there," I respond as he wraps an Ace bandage around my thigh and then puts an ice pack on before wrapping me up more to hold it against my thigh.

"Let's get your leg up." He helps me position myself on the bench so I'm laying down. He puts a cooler under my knee and hands me a few towels for under my head. Kody helps position them for me.

"Kody!" Coach Steele barks. "Get out here and show Hatford how the fuck this is done!"

Kody rolls his eyes before turning and jogging towards the field. "Shouldn't have taken me out, Coach," he says smoothly, but I can hear the bite behind the words.

"You just earned yourself laps, Remington!" Coach snaps.

"Yeah, yeah!" Kody rumbles as he jogs towards the line and takes his position.

"Fuck me," I say shaking my head at his attitude as I close my eyes.

A few minutes later, a shadow crosses over my sun, and I open one eye. I grin. "Hey, Racer."

"Hey, Drake. How's the leg?"

"Not bad. Just doing what the trainer says. I want back on the field before the end of the season. Where's Blade?"

"Uh. Waiting. Somewhere. I'm just here to take you there." He grins a little wickedly.

I open both eyes curiously. "Where is he?"

"Sworn to secrecy, man. Can't help you."

I laugh. "Sounds like Blade. They should be almost done. We'll hit the showers, then I'll meet you outside."

"Did you drive here?"

"Yeah. I actually took my bike. I haven't ridden it in a while, but it felt like a good day to do it."

"Well, then I'll lead you. How's the bike running?"

"I think it needs some more work done, but it's getting there, and I'm getting better about riding it. It's a lot more fun than before for sure."

"We'll get it in the shop and see what's up with it. Talk about what you want done."

"Hit the showers!" Coach commands. "Except you, Kody. Take your laps! Good job today, everyone!"

I can feel the ice in Kody's glare from where I am as the trainer helps me sit up and starts unwrapping my thigh.

"What the fuck was that?" Racer asks.

I shake my head. "Not a clue. This has been an all year thing. And a last year thing. We can't figure it out, and we're in our second year on the team under the same coach. No one gets it."

"Huh. Well, okay, I'll meet you in the parking lot."

"Won't be long." I head for the locker room curious about what Blade has planned, and confused as fuck over Kody's behavior.

☪ ☪ ☪

I pull into the small parking lot of Envious Inked Escape where Racer's wife and Blade's sister works. Lizzie is incredible. Her work is truly second to none.

I park my bike next to Racer's and follow him inside the small shop. When I see Blade, I grin and step into his waiting arms.

"I missed you," he rumbles. "And I have a surprise for you." He pulls back but keeps his arms around me.

"Consider my curiosity peaked. What's up?"

"Well, remember how we were talking about ring tattoos instead of rings because the rings are too obvious to the fact there's someone special in my life?"

I raise an eyebrow, my heart starting to race. I grip the back of his shirt a little tighter, bunching it in my fist. "Yeah...?"

He glances around and gestures just as Lizzie comes out from a back room. "How 'bout now?"

I blink. "Are you... proposing...?" I'm about to swallow my heart, but I'm vibrating with anxiousness. I want him to say yes so badly. Racer slips his arm around Lizzie. They both smile.

Blade grins and slowly drops to one knee as he holds my hands in his. "Drake, we've been together for a while. Technically before we were legally allowed, but neither of us have ever been afraid to break rules." He kisses both of my hands but keeps his eyes locked on mine. "I've never wanted to tie myself to anyone, but then you came along and obliterated all my walls. I was so fucking possessive of you. I still am. The thought of you being with anyone else kills me. I don't have a lot to give you. Hell, I won't even give you a church ceremony or religious anything. All I can give you is me. My heart. Soul. And a promise that I'll love you for the rest of time." He releases one of my hands and looks to Lizzie as he holds out a hand. It's then I realize she's holding a leather jacket with Viper's Venom cuts.

"Oh my God," I whisper.

"You earned this. You earned this in so many different ways. You respect the crew. You put them and family above all else and actively work to protect them without taking advantage of anyone. But the biggest way is by loving me, sticking by me, and never letting me give up. Never letting me give you up. Marry me, baby. Please." He stays on his knee but holds up the jacket as if it's a ring.

I take it and stare at it teary. The patch says 'Member', meaning I'm not a prospect just waiting to be part of the club. I'm already in it, but the symbolism is so much more than that. It means I'm not on the outside looking in. I'm not one fuck up away from being kicked out. I'm in it. I'm part of it.

I'm part of him.

That's what I care about. I'm part of him. I'm by his side through it all. It's truly a ride or die situation. I belong to the crew, but mostly, I belong to him.

I put the jacket on over my t-shirt and instantly feel even closer to him. "I'll marry you," I almost whisper.

Racer and Lizzie cheer. Blade stands and wraps his arms around me. I hug him as he buries his face in my neck and kisses it. "I thought we could design our own ring tattoos . Lizzie could do them."

I'm choked up and beyond touched. So many emotions are flowing through me, and I don't know what to do with them. So, before I can think about it anymore, I take his hand as I pull away and drag him towards a room with a door. It's either the office or a bathroom. Maybe a supply room. I don't care. I need five minutes alone with him to get my emotions in check. He's the only one who knows how to center me when I can't figure out what the fuck I'm thinking.

Once I get into the room, I slam the door behind us and find a light on the wall. I quickly look around. It's a supply closet, and Blade is a little shocked.

"What are you doing, baby?" he rumbles deeply.

"I don't know." I put my hands against my temples. "I'm thinking a million things. How much I love you. How much I want to marry you right fucking now. Get a priest. Do the rings. The fact that this jacket represents so much more than me being accepted into the crew. It's really a testament of our love and your desire to have me by your side. Truly. Fuck, Blade." I drop my hands and just look at him. "I can't even grasp one thought. I'm happy. Excited. Ecstatic. I want to shout this from the rooftops, but I'm scared at how fast I want it to move. I'm not scared of any of it. Just how fast I want it to happen. Am I crazy? What the -"

Blade presses a hand against my mouth. The other grips the back of my neck. "Stop. Nothing is wrong with you. You're not crazy. We both know what we want. We know it's right. Speed has nothing to do with it." He takes his hand away from my mouth and presses his lips to mine, but it doesn't have the calming effect it should. Inside, it ignites me and makes me want to climb him.

So, I let my body take control and do just that. I press myself closer to him. I try pushing him back against a wall, but he doesn't budge.

74

He reads me like a damn book and immediately knows just what I need, even though I don't have a damn clue.

Blade pulls away and pushes me to my knees with one hand. The other undoes the belt of his jeans. Seconds later, his button is undone. He unzips his fly and reaches for his dick. My eyes get heavy with lust when he pulls it out. His fingers tangle in my hair, and I open my mouth. He pumps his massive length a few times and teases me with his tip, only letting my tongue dart out to lick it. He doesn't let me move. He doesn't let me suck. Just lick.

"Quiet," he demands. I nod. "Look up at me."

I do as I'm told and fall instantly into the submissive role he expects and I need to show. I'm tired of being the strong one. "Yes, sir," I say just above a whisper. I know Racer and Lizzie won't let anyone in here, but I still don't want anyone any wiser of what's happening, even though they know. I want to please my Dom. I want to please Blade.

He slowly pushes his dick into my mouth, but I don't close around him. I don't lick. I do nothing but watch him and enjoy the feel of him sliding into me; his taste. "Suck," he rumbles. His dick twitches.

I leave my hands at my sides and let him completely take control of the pace. If he wants me to stroke him, he'll tell me, and that's what I need. I need to leave all control at his feet so he can center me.

I keep my eyes trained on his and suck his dick like it's a fucking sucker. I flick my tongue around his tip, and when he pulls out, I lightly scrape my teeth along his length. He groans low and lets out a satisfied breath as he thrusts in and out of my mouth guiding my head to meet his pace.

"Fuck yeah, baby," he whispers as his head falls back. "Good boy. Just like that." He looks back at me. His dangerous eyes sparkle. I look up at him through my lashes and suck harder. I moan low when his tip hits the back of my throat.

My dick gets harder and harder. I want to touch it, but I'm enjoying how it feels straining against my jeans. I adjust it so it doesn't hurt, but all of my attention is on Blade and making him feel as pleasured as I possibly can. I leave my hand on my dick, though, and give it a couple of squeezes. Each moan that rumbles from my throat hits his dick and sends vibrations through it. I know it does because it's what he does to me.

He thrusts faster into my mouth and holds me still. I suck him, and each time he hits the back of my throat, I swallow while swirling my tongue over his dick. His quiet moans and sighs show me I'm doing it right, and before long, I feel him thickening.

"I'm gonna come, baby. Swallow for me," he commands in a whisper. I can hear the dominance still and nod so he knows I understand. He thrusts a couple more times before I feel his tangy taste sliding down my throat. I moan and swallow everything he gives me. "Oh fuck, Drake. Fuck, baby. Take all of it. Good boy."

I give my dick a few more squeezes as I lick him clean, knowing he'll make sure I'm very well taken care of soon. Once I finish, he helps me stand and kisses me while he's putting himself away. I melt into him like he's all I need to breathe.

He pulls away gently as he squeezes my cock and drops to his knees. "Let me take care of this."

He unbuttons my jeans and unzips them. Moments later, he's sucking me off so hard, my eyes roll back in my head. I come so fast, I barely know what's happening. All I feel is him swallowing my come as I hold onto his shoulders.

A few moments after my heartbeat finally slows, I notice that all of the chaos I was feeling just a few minutes ago is gone. I feel calm and centered once more, just like he always makes me feel.

"I love you," I whisper to him as he pulls off my dick and stands. He helps me put myself away. I button my jeans and zip them as he kisses me..

He pulls away slowly, takes my hand, and leads me out of the supply closet. "I love you, too."

"Ready to tell me what you guys want so we can get it all designed?" Lizzie asks us with a giant smile.

"Yeah," I say, confident in everything once more. "Yeah. We're ready."

She squeals as we all sit down. Blade doesn't let go of my hand as we hash out what we want. The more time passes, the more relaxed I feel. I'm getting married to the love of my life, the one who makes me feel whole.

The one who makes me feel like I can fly and crash land without getting the least bit hurt.

The one who entered my life when I needed him the most and protected me when I didn't know I needed to be.

The one who gave me hope.

Chapter Thirteen

☪ Blade ☪

(Two Weeks Later)

"In front of friends and family, blood and not, and by the power this great state of Texas has given to me, I declare the two of you husband and husband," Reverend, and older member of Viper's Venom who is in his late sixties, says with a huge grin.

The guy is as Atheist as they come but got his name because he's truly just a good guy who wants to live his life on the right side of the line. He became ordained to perform ceremonies long ago because many people closest to him, mainly those in the crew, don't believe in God, or, like me, have one fucked up relationship with him. Others are outright Satanists, but Reverend don't care. He believes everyone has the right to love who they want and enjoy a ceremony if they want without hassle.

That's what Drake wanted. Well, mostly his family. Kody's parents, specifically. Not because they want to push religion, but because they want their nephew to experience everything a wedding involves right down to the ceremony.

"Come on, now, Prez. Kiss your groom!" Reverend says.

I grin and tug Drake close. I wrap an arm around his waist. The other, I curl around the back of his neck so I can control the kiss. I lean in and press my lips to his. He moans into my mouth and closes his eyes. His arms wrap around me, and I deepen the kiss. It's powerful. The sparks that always ignite when we're near each other explode. Instead of blowing us apart like it should, we only meld together, like we're soldered to one another.

Cheers and applause erupts behind us, but as my tongue swipes over his, the noise is drowned out. All I hear is our tongues and lips clashing. The only thing I feel is his body against mine; his dick pressing against my own length.

I force myself to pull away before I can't stop myself from taking it further right here in front of everyone. Drake sways a little as he opens his eyes and smiles up at me, eyes shining with love. We're both wearing the same thing, jeans with a white t-shirt and our leather vest with our patches, but I could stare at Drake all day long and think he's the sexiest man I've ever seen. It doesn't matter what he wears, but looking at him in his cuts is enough to make a man weak.

I take his hand, and we turn towards the whistles and clapping. We didn't do the traditional one side for his family and one side for mine. Bikers are mixed with men and women in dressier clothing than just jeans and cuts, but everyone is happy. It turned out to be a larger event than we thought it would be, but it doesn't matter because everyone who is here are people who mean everything to us.

I lead Drake to our friends and our family. All of his teammates are here. He's back to playing fully now. We share hugs and handshakes as everyone mingles and congratulates us. While that's going on, we have people not far away on the grill. We've decided we're not catering. Instead, we're doing a traditional Texas barbecue complete with pork belly and cornbread. We're doing burnt ends and beef brisket as well as pecan pie and barbecue chicken. We even threw in some Tex-Mex and made sure there's a Texas sheet cake. There's something for everyone.

Everything is starting to smell delicious. People start heading for the tents we've set up, but I keep Drake back. I turn to him and brush his slightly unruly hair back from his eyes. "We did it."

Drake smiles and nods. "We really did it. I've never been so happy. I thought X got married a bit young, but fuck. He was right. When you know, you just know." He steps closer and grips my vest as he kisses me. "And I know."

I grin. "I've always known. From the second I laid eyes on you, I knew you were mine." I bring his hand to my lips and kiss the ring tattoo. We got matching ones. His says my name. Mine says his. They both wrap around our finger in a barbed wire style that represents how getting to us and breaking us will tear anyone who tries it apart. We're unbreakable.

"I'd say this is the first day of the rest of our lives, but I'd be wrong. The first day of the rest of our lives was the day you saved mine."

I lean in and kiss him again before pulling away slowly and leading him to the tents. We've set up air conditioning inside them to make sure people stay cool in the Texas heat. It may be October, but it's still fucking hot.

Once we get inside, the air feels instantly different. Light and cool. People are talking and laughing. Someone started playing music. We didn't hire a DJ so the music is coming from a stereo one of my crew hooked up. If there's one thing consistent about all biker crews, it's that we all love to drink and party. There's plenty of food and alcohol for everyone. We'll probably even have stuff left.

Drake is pulled away by several people on the way to our table, but he keeps dragging me with him. I'm introduced to a lot of his friends and teammates as well as several people from Chicago that I'll never remember the names of. When we finally get to our table after getting our food, I've never been more happy.

"Fuck me, I'm starving," I rumble.

"I could eat an entire cow," Drake agrees.

I grin as we eat and converse with people who come up to us. There's a sense of real peace that I haven't felt in a long time. I know there's shit looming on the horizon, but the fact that we've gotten so far with the mystery surrounding Drake's parents' death is something I'm thankful we've been able to accomplish.

We've discovered that the information uncovered by Drake's father and mother was a sex trafficking ring that did involve people in the city. A small motel seemed to have been the center. Colton led a task force that took down the owner of the motel and ended up saving some girls who were there. It led them to finding a hideout where other girls were being held.

Sloane hasn't given up her article yet. She's still working on a hunch that this is all bigger than just the small bust that Colton got out of it. She believes it's connected to this Anonymous person. We know he called several of the gang members several times, but it's always been from a different number. A burner phone. We haven't gotten any further with that. Colton also got the bust for taking down Santos Del Infierno. He was able to get a lot of charges against most of them, trafficking included. Heartbreaking because they were all so young.

Some were let go because there was nothing they could be held on, but I'm pretty sure they've all been scared shitless coming up against three different crews. They all thought they were going to be shot on sight. It was enough to put them on a different path. At least, that's the hope. So far, so good.

The two who did kill Drake's parents, though, are going down for a very long time for first degree murder. Drake and all of his cousins took the news of it being Remy and Buckley behind all of that as we had expected. No one really seemed that surprised. It looks like Drake's parents knew there was a hit on them. That was some of the information that Lance was able to uncover in files he was able to extract from whatever sources he has. The guy scares me. I don't ask how he does shit. Turns out, though, that they were going to Jay Calvary for help, as we knew, but also for protection.

Drake found it ironic that his parents seemed to be aware of all of the stuff his uncles were involved in before anyone else actually did. The only thing that got him a little down about all of this is how different things could've been if his parents had been able to get that information to Jay. He knows that it wasn't all of the information they had. He spiraled some and wondered if knowing what his parents did would've stopped so many of the events that have happened over the past couple of years. Not only their deaths, but also Xavier's and Brant's issues with their fathers. He believed it could've stopped Xavier from getting into a fight with his dad and Sloane from getting beaten up and kidnapped by Brant's dad.

In the end, though, he knows he can't spiral down that dark hole. Wondering if things would've been different is okay, but obsessing over just how different things could've been if one single thing didn't happen, isn't. Besides, as painful as it is, had any of this not happened, I may never have known him. Drake and I come from two very, very different worlds.

After everyone is fed, the real party begins. There's dancing and a lot of laughing, but the one thing that stands out to me is Drake in my arms. Fast or slow songs don't matter. We move to the beat of the music playing in our hearts. We hold each other close and share a lot of kisses that leave us both straining against our jeans.

"Do you think Kody has a thing for Coach Steele?" Drake asks me out of the blue, snapping me back to reality before I take him somewhere where we can both suck each other's dick.

I clear my throat and glance to where Kody is glaring at their coach, who's with some blonde woman I've never seen in my life. "Uh… I don't know, baby. I didn't think he swung our way."

"Neither did I. He's got a girl with him all the damn time, but so did Xavier. I mean, Kody's date tonight is one of the cheerleaders at the university. It's just that he hates the coach with a fucking passion. It borders on something else entirely. Like right now. The chick he's with is all over him, but his eyes are on the coach."

I pay a little more attention to the two. Coach Steele smiles at his date right before she kisses him. Kody looks like he's about to snap as he gently pushes away from the girl he's with and storms out of the tent.

"Huh," I say in surprise.

"See?" Drake says. The coach pulls away from the kiss very abruptly as he watches Kody a little too closely. He looks like he's about to get up but thinks better of it when he sees Kody's date chasing after. "Don't tell me that wasn't weird."

"Definitely weird, but I don't know what to make of it, Dray."

Drake grumbles as we go back to dancing. He rests his head on my shoulder and lets out a sigh as he relaxes. I hold him closer to me and continue to sway with him.

The party continues long into the night. By the time the sun starts coming up the next morning, there are people passed out in truck beds and in their vehicles. Some left to go home or to a hotel, but a lot stayed. Cole and Dylan are awake and snuggled together watching the sunrise and leaning against the side of the clubhouse. Drake and I aren't far from them. It's the best seat on the compound to see the sun come up.

"Thank you for making this so special and memorable," Drake says sleepily.

"You don't ever need to thank me, baby. My job is to take care of you and make sure you always have everything you want and need."

"And to love me."

"Always to love you." I hug him tighter.

As the sun rises on the horizon, I can't help but feel like it's a symbol of my life with Drake. New but steady. Fresh but dependable. While I don't know what the days ahead of us will bring, I do know one thing.

Just as the sun will always rise, Drake and I will always be by each other's sides.

Together, just like we were always meant to me.

The End

Coming Soon In The Forbidden Temptation Series

The Forbidden Temptation Series continues with *The Coach's Forbidden Temptation*.

After suffering a career ending knee injury, I'm forced to retire from the Chicago Guardians, the pro NFL team I've played with for fifteen years. To say it was heartbreaking is the understatement of the century. Even though I've had a great career, I find my way back to my hometown of Brystone Springs, Texas.

Brystone Springs University, where I've taken a coaching job, is where the trouble begins. I didn't know that one of the team's All-Stars is the man I had a mind-blowing one-night stand with when I first got back to town. Now, I have to see him every damn day.

Kody Remington.

He's stubborn, sassy, and intoxicating as hell. His looks and memories of that night haunt me every waking and sleeping moment. His attitude, though, is appalling and makes me want to take him over my knee. I can't touch him again, though. Not if I want to keep my job, and he wants to stay in school.

One day, everything changes. Suddenly, I don't give a damn about the consequences. I know we both need each other. What I don't know is if our intense feelings for one another are strong enough to save us both from forces I don't even understand.

Order your copy of *The Coach's Forbidden Temptation* today!

The Forbidden Temptation Series

Available Now

The Detective's Forbidden Temptation
The Running Back's Forbidden Temptation

Other Books By Melony Ann
The Beautiful Dream Series

Available Now

Loving You
My Love, My Heart
Softening Lyric
Undercover Temptations
Captain Charming
Breaking Boundaries
Crashing Into You
Tactical Inferno
Ravishing Our Queen
Cherished By The Texan
Unveiling Our Passions

Box Sets Available

The Beautiful Dream Series: Box Set: Part 1
The Beautiful Dream Series: Box Set: Part 2

The Crane Family Series

Available Now

The Reluctant Mafia King
Sweet Lies
Billion Dollar Love Story
Be Mine
Protecting Her
Dangerously Forbidden Love
His Heart
Love In The Dark

Box Sets Available

The Crane Family Series

The Deimos Trilogy

Available Now

Connor's Legacy
Aryan's Alpha
Kade's Redemption

Box Sets Available

The Deimos Trilogy

The Lucinio Family Series

Available Now

Rising From The Ashes
The Player's Rebel
Encrypting My Heart
Fighting My Fate
Phoenix Rising
Defending Her Honor

Multi Author Series
Piper Falls: Firehouse 49

Available Now

Ignite My Fire by Melony Ann
Regain My Fire by Kindra White
Playing With My Fire by D.L. Howe
Fight My Fire by Darley Collins
Against My Fire by Anneke Boshoff
Relight My Fire by Louise Murchie
Harness My Fire by Ayana Lisbet
Quench My Fire by Havana Wilder

Let's Be Friends

Follow me on

Bookbub

Facebook

Goodreads

Instagram

Tik Tok

Visit my website
www.melonyannauthor.com

Subscribe to my newsletter and get a FREE never-seen-before NOVELLA
just for subscribers!
https://www.melonyannauthor.com/exclusive-content

Join my Facebook Reader Group!
Melony Ann's Sizzling Book Nook

The official Forbidden Temptation Series Playlist on YouTube
https://youtube.com/playlist?list=PLGEiD5wbQmDfSjcIbdaBUl79mqR6t
URPP

Dedication

When the sun and moon no longer shine, your light will still guide us home.

Acknowledgements

Brad - I just realized Shameless by Garth Brooks is on this playlist. I don't remember putting it on there, but I love it because it's one of your favorites. You've never been shy about your love for us, and we'll never be shy about ours for you.

Laura - Every time I hear Perfect by Ed Sheeran and Beyonce, I think of you. Specifically the part where they talk about being barefoot on the grass while listening to their favorite song. You're my dark angel. I don't deserve you, but I'll forever cherish you and keep you snuggled close.

Jay - Out of the blue, I'll sometimes remember a random thing you said or did, and it brings a smile to my face. And all of the sudden, I remember just why I fell for the tall and really hot guy in a military uniform while sitting in an airport terminal nervous out of my mind for my first flight by myself.

Anneke - You know when you just meet someone and click with them, and then you become so close, it's like you're family? Oh. Right. Of course you do because that's literally us. Laura and I love you!

Jason - Sometimes, I don't think you're real. You're so incredibly different from everyone I've ever come in contact with. You always make me feel like I'm special and important, even when I'm so low that I don't think I can come out of it. You're so down to earth, it's unnerving, but I love everything about you.

Kayla - When a person is broken, sometimes, another soul comes out of nowhere to console them and put them back together. I'm not sure where I'd be without you to bark at me when I think I'm sucking it up, but I'm glad for you!

To the Bookstagram Community.

To my family.

To all of those who believe in me and support me.

To all of those who don't.

Cover by: Carter Cover Designs

Edited by: Alyssa Skaggs

About Melony Ann

Melony Ann began writing short stories and poetry as a child. She continued honing her craft over the years until she took the plunge and began publishing her work, despite having severe anxiety.

Melony writes contemporary romance stories that are full of suspense and a lot of steam.

When she isn't writing, she is loving her family and working to make her life something she deserves.

Melony believes that if her writing can inspire just one person, then all of her hard work is worth it.

Her hope is that her writing allows each and every one of her readers to escape for a little while. To dive into a different world one book at a time.

www.ingramcontent.com/pod-product-compliance
Lightning Source LLC
Chambersburg PA
CBHW051311170626
46809CB00004B/1844